# WHERE THE CROWN FELL

## The Rise of a Forgotten Heir

### Winter Warleggan

# Table Of Contents

# Copyright

## About The Author

Winter Warleggan has loved fantasy novels for as long as she can remember. At 17, she began writing the story that would one day become her debut novel—never imagining it would actually make it to print. Over the years, she returned to the manuscript time and again, quietly shaping it while life moved on. With the support of friends and family, she finally brought the story to life and into the world. Winter lives in Gainsborough, a small town in Lincolnshire, England, where she raises her tween daughter and continues to write the kind of books she's always loved.

## Author's Note

What started as a dream—a flicker of an idea born in the quiet hours—grew into something far greater than I ever imagined. Life carried me through many twists and turns, but this world, these characters, always lived in my heart.

I feel I owe it to that younger version of myself to finish what I started. This book is for her—for the girl who believed in magic, in love, in courage—and never let go of the story.

— Winter Warleggan

\*\*\*

# Prologue

*Long before the crown fell, before the names of kings were etched into marble and erased by blood, there was a prophecy—whispered in candlelit crypts and buried beneath layers of dust and denial.*

*"When the child of the forgotten bloodline rises beneath a broken dawn, the kingdoms shall tremble, and the rightful heir shall claim what was stolen."*

*Most called it myth. A tale spun by mad seers and forest witches who once served the old gods. But in the highest tower of the royal court, a queen once burned the scroll that bore those words and ordered silence upon pain of death.*

*She knew.*

*She knew her son had loved a woman unfit for thrones and that the child they bore in secret would threaten everything—every alliance, every throne, every lie.*

*So she buried the truth with banishment and blades.*

*But truth does not die in exile.*

*It survives in shadows. In daughters raised among birch trees. In the rising ache of something long denied.*

*And now, beneath another broken dawn, the forgotten*

WINTER WARLEGGAN

*blood stirs once more.*

# CHAPTER 1 -
# BROKEN DAWN

The sun had only just begun to spill its pale light across the horizon when Eleanor stepped out of the cottage. She was tall and lithe, with blonde waves spilling past her shoulders, plump lips and green-grey eyes set above a narrow waist and gently rounded hips —an hourglass silhouette that could turn heads anywhere. The morning mist clung low to the ground like a final breath. The birch trees whispered in the breeze, their slender silver trunks stretching like guardians into the sky. Their rustling leaves sounded like voices—soft, mourning. Inside, the fire had long since died to embers, but Eleanor didn't dare rekindle it.


Her mother, Zara, still breathed. Barely.

Eleanor returned inside, her palms wrapped around a fresh cloth soaked in cold stream water. She knelt beside the cot, gently pressing it against Zara's forehead. Her mother's skin was clammy, feverish, pale as linen.

Zara stirred, blinking weakly. "Morning already?" Her once-dark hair was shot through with silver at the temples, framing high cheekbones above a strong jaw; though fever-pale and fragile now, the proud lift of her shoulders and the steady intelligence in her grey-green eyes still spoke of the woman who had once been Queen's confidante.


"It's still early," Eleanor whispered. "Rest."

Zara gave the faintest shake of her head. "No time for resting, my storm. We have little left, you and I. I must speak while I still can."

Eleanor's lips pressed into a familiar ache. They'd had this talk before—countless times, in fragments and stolen hours—but the weight of it never grew lighter.


"You remember what I told you," Zara continued, voice rough with the strain. "How the Queen banished me, not for treason or theft—but for love.

Because I dared to care for someone above my station."

Eleanor nodded. She knew every detail.

"He wasn't a king back then," Zara went on, "just a prince—young, defiant, and too foolish to hide what we were. We thought we were clever. Careful. But the Queen saw the change in me. She always did. She saw the way he looked at me, how he stopped seeking other matches."

"She saw the child before he did," Eleanor whispered.

Zara's eyes fluttered shut for a moment. "She gave me a choice—disappear quietly or be executed publicly. So I ran. Pregnant and alone, through the Outlands. She thought I wouldn't survive. She sent guards to ensure I wouldn't."

"But you did."

"I did," Zara said. "Because I had you."

She reached shakily for the pouch tied to her waist and placed it into Eleanor's hands. Inside were a handful of letters, pressed lavender petals, and a pendant—a golden crest with a stag beneath a rising sun.

"The sigil of Wonderworth," Zara murmured. "It belonged to your father. He never knew what she did. Never knew you existed. He couldn't stop her—not then. He was powerless against his mother."

Eleanor turned it over slowly in her palm, the weight of it anchoring her breath. "He doesn't even know me."

Zara's voice cracked. "But he deserves to. And the kingdom deserves the truth. You have his strength, Eleanor—but your path is your own. Go to him. Not to reclaim a place—but to claim yourself."

Outside, a mourning dove called out once, twice. Zara's breathing slowed.

"Mama," Eleanor whispered, brushing a strand of sweat-dampened hair from her mother's brow. The lantern light caught the ache in Zara's fine lines—the slight hollow at her temples, the trembling curve of her lips—remnants of the fierce grace that had carried her through court intrigues.

Zara's voice was barely a whisper. "Promise me you'll go. Promise me you'll find Wonderworth… and remind the world who you are."

Eleanor leaned forward, her lips trembling against her mother's ear. "I promise."

Zara's lips curled in the faintest smile. Her chest rose once more—and then fell.

And did not rise again.

\*\*\*

By midmorning, the sun had pierced through the mist, and Eleanor stood by the base of the old birch, hands blistered from digging. She had laid her mother's body to rest wrapped in the blanket Zara had woven herself, pressed lavender tucked beneath her arms.

"I'll be brave," Eleanor said, placing the final stone on the grave. Her voice cracked. "I'll find him."

Footsteps approached from behind. Old Marnie, from the ridge above, had come down the slope with her walking stick and a basket of herbs she didn't seem to care about anymore.

"She's resting now," the old woman said gently. "And you've got a storm ahead of you."

"I don't know the way," Eleanor whispered.

"You do," Marnie said. "You just don't want to believe it."

Eleanor looked up, the wind catching her braid and tugging it across her face. "The Outlands, Marnie. I have to go through the Outlands."

The woman didn't answer at first. She took a long breath, settling herself beside Eleanor with a slow grunt. "That cursed forest," she said finally.

"There's not a soul who passes through that place unchanged."

"They say the trees whisper to each other," Eleanor said. "They say time moves different inside."

"They say worse," Marnie replied. "They say men go mad. That something lives in there. Not beast, not man. Shadows that can take your skin."

Eleanor nodded grimly. "I used to think it was all just stories."

"They were warnings. Every kingdom has one tale or another. But none dare claim the Outlands. And that should tell you enough."

She reached into her satchel and pulled out a brittle parchment scroll. She unrolled it slowly to reveal a faded map: six kingdoms like petals around a dark centre.

"Look here," she said, pointing. "You're here, in Thaloria, at the western bend of the River Orwain. Just past the banks lies the edge of the forest. Cross it, and you enter Taryn—stone-hearted and dangerous, but crossable if you stay sharp. From there, you'll find your way to Wonderworth. That's where you're going."

Eleanor followed the lines of ink with her eyes. "What about Isendra?"

"Closed. Civil war's torn her in half. No roads left, and they're shooting anything that moves near their borders. Forget Isendra."

"Could I sail around the Outlands?" Eleanor asked, though she knew the answer.

"No." Marnie's voice turned grave. "The Waterlock Treaty saw to that. Every kingdom signed it—no boats beyond the river that rings the Outlands. They feared foreign invaders. Feared what might creep through if the waters weren't watched."

"So... no land route. No sea passage. Just the forest."

"Aye. And beyond it, all your truths."

Eleanor folded the map slowly and tucked it inside her cloak. The pouch from her mother weighed heavily against her chest.

"I'll go," she said, quieter now. "Through the Outlands."

Marnie handed her a flask and a pouch of dried root. "For luck," she said. "And for memory."

Eleanor looked toward the trees in the east—dark, tall, and twisting. A world of horrors between her and the only family she had left.

But she would go. Because now there was nothing left to keep her.

# CHAPTER 2 - INTO
# THE OUTLANDS

The night before her departure, Eleanor could not sleep.

Grief clung to her skin like damp wool, heavy and close. She moved through the cottage like a ghost herself, laying out provisions by the pale amber glow of a lantern: strips of smoked meat, dried bitterroots, a waterskin, and her mother's healing herbs—still fragrant in the leather pouch tied with twine. She sharpened the old dagger Zara had kept in the spice drawer and wrapped her cloak in oiled cloth to protect it from the rot-heavy mists she'd been warned about since childhood.

Every movement was deliberate. Every silence was filled with memory. Outside, the forest edge loomed like a promise no one wanted kept.

In the village, they used to whisper about the Outlands as if speaking its name too loudly might draw it closer. It was not just a forest—it was a scar across the world. A place older than kings and darker than night. They said it twisted those who entered it, bent them into shadows of themselves, or worse—made them forget what they were entirely. Those who returned came back different. Wrong. And most never came back at all.

Eleanor had seen that fear in Marnie's eyes. She carried it now in her bones.

But she had made a promise. To her mother. To herself. And to the bloodline she barely understood.

As dawn crept into the sky like breath upon glass, Eleanor stood at the edge of the River Orwain. The water gleamed silver in the first light, broad and swift, slicing through the land like a barrier between the known and the damned. She found the old rowboat moored where Marnie had said it would be, just beneath the willow's reach. The wood was damp but sturdy. She climbed in and untied it with trembling fingers.

The crossing was slow. Mist rose from the water, clinging to her lashes and cloak. Each stroke of the oar sounded too loud in the silence. When she reached the far bank, she dragged the boat onto shore and stood motionless.

On the far bank, the world changed.
The air was different—damp, electric, wrong. Trees towered in unnatural silence, their trunks furred with dark moss, their branches reaching like clawed hands. Fog coiled low to the ground, thick and moving with a will of its own. No birdsong. No chirp of insect. Only stillness.

Eleanor drew her cloak tighter around her shoulders. She stepped into the trees.
The Outlands swallowed the world behind her.

She walked for what felt like hours, senses taut. The path dissolved into thorns and uneven ground, forcing her to navigate with growing unease. The mist shifted constantly, like it was breathing. Shadows moved just beyond sight.
Then—
A sound. Low. Wet. Breathing.

Eleanor froze.

A figure slithered through the fog ahead. It was not walking. It dragged itself forward—limbs too long, too many joints. Its head twitched violently from side to side, and its body pulsed with a sickly amber light that glowed beneath stretched, translucent skin. Where its eyes should have been, clusters of glimmering black orbs blinked at her—dozens of them, each moving independently.

It opened its mouth—or what passed for one. It split sideways, a vertical maw that ran from jaw to collarbone, revealing glistening teeth that looked carved from broken glass.

Then came the sound. A scream that wasn't a scream—metal tearing, air splitting, blood freezing.

Eleanor stumbled back.

The creature charged.

She ran.

Branches whipped at her face. Roots snatched at her feet. She tripped once, caught herself, pushed forward. The shriek echoed through the trees, impossibly close.

It moved fast. Faster than it should have.

She caught glimpses of it through the fog—limbs

contorting unnaturally, dragging itself sideways, then leaping upright. Its mouths opened and closed in hunger. There were more than one. She could hear them. Dozens of steps, wrong and mismatched.

One leapt at her from the side.
She screamed, ducked, and rolled, just as it collided with a tree. Bark exploded. The thing righted itself, too quickly, its neck bending backward like a hinge.

She threw a rock. It didn't flinch.
Another lunged from the shadows. It hit her hard. Her back slammed into a root knot. Her dagger flew from her grasp.
Its breath was rot and bile. One of its eyes blinked inches from her face. A mouth on its shoulder opened wide.

She screamed.

And then, from the mist—
A burst of silver light.

The silver fox.
It moved like wind over water, a blur of moonlight and fury. It struck the creature with silent precision. The beast shrieked and recoiled as its

flesh sizzled against the fox's touch.

The fox circled Eleanor once, then stood between her and the creature, eyes glowing like stars. Another beast stepped into the clearing. The fox met it head-on.

The clearing exploded with light. The beasts screamed and scattered, some disintegrating into mist, others fleeing into the dark.

Eleanor could only watch, breath shallow, chest tight.

The fox turned and padded to her side. It nudged her hand gently. Its touch was warm.

Then it vanished into the trees.

She lay still for a long while. Her body ached. Her hands trembled.

She had survived.

She retrieved her dagger, blood-streaked and cracked.

The forest behind her was quiet again—but not empty. Never empty.

She stood and moved forward, wounded but alive.

But the Outlands were not finished with her.

Just beyond the next bend, where the fog grew thick as wool and the light thinned to ash, something stirred. A new presence. Slower. Heavier.

A second beast.
This one did not charge.
It emerged from the trees like a shadow made flesh —taller than the first, easily twice her height, with antler-like protrusions crowning its head, each one dripping with moss and blood. Its limbs were too long, ending in talons that scraped the earth as it walked. Beneath its hooded brow, a single eye glowed red—not flickering like fire, but steady, ancient.

It spoke.
Its voice crawled through the trees like oil and ice.

"Daughter of Zara."
Eleanor froze. Every hair on her neck rose. Her blood turned to glass.

"You are not meant to be here yet," it said. "But you came. And now you are seen."

She took a step back. Her legs threatened to buckle.

"What are you?" she whispered.
It smiled.

The mouth split upward this time, vertical and impossibly wide. Its breath was colder than snowmelt and smelled of decay and iron.

"I am what follows. I am what waits. I am the shape beneath the skin of your world."
She ran.
This time, the chase was silent. No shrieks. No snapping branches. Just the whisper of her own breath and the faint thud of her feet. But she could feel it behind her—gliding rather than running, never faster, but always just near.

She slipped once on wet moss, fell hard. The air rushed from her lungs.

The creature loomed above her.
Its head tilted, studying her. "I will remember your scent," it said. "You will remember mine."

Then—
A flare of silver.

The fox again. Fiercer. Brighter. It did not attack this time. It stepped between them, and the space warped with light and heat.

The beast hissed. Not in fear. In recognition.

"Old thing," it said to the fox. "Still guarding lost causes."

The fox bared its teeth, glowing with starlight.

The beast faded, step by step, into the fog. But before it vanished, it whispered toward Eleanor:

"We will meet again, girl. When the moon dies."

Then it was gone.

Eleanor lay there, heart racing, lungs heaving. She was shaking uncontrollably.

The fox touched its nose to her forehead, then disappeared without a sound.

When she finally stood again, she knew something had changed.

That voice—that presence—stayed with her like a brand. She would dream of it for months. And when she heard whispers of beasts returning in Wonderworth, that voice would echo in her sleep.

She did not yet know that the creature she met would return in fire and fury.

But some part of her understood: it had marked her.

The Outlands had shown her its nightmare. And she had walked through it.

Wonderworth lay ahead.
And it owed her its attention.

***

The clearing faded behind her as Eleanor pressed forward, the light of dawn breaking across a
land very different from the one she'd left behind.

Taryn greeted her with jagged cliffs and ash-coloured skies, the terrain hard and weather-worn. The trees here were stunted, their leaves grey-green, their roots knotted into stone. The wind no longer whispered but howled—restless, wild, and unkind. Even the birds here called
with rough, scraping cries.
This was a country carved by survival, where kindness was rare and everything cost something.

Eleanor walked for hours, her boots caked in dust, her legs sore from strain. Just as the sun tipped toward evening, she saw smoke curling in the sky—thin and steady. Not fire, but
hearth. Hope.

She followed it.

It led her to a crooked little cottage nestled at the base of a hill. Vines curled around its chimney, and chickens clucked lazily in a crooked coop.

Outside, a woman stood stirring a pot over an open flame, her apron streaked with ash and broth. Her hair was silver and coarse, tied back with twine. Her eyes, sharp and clever, narrowed as Eleanor approached.

"Lost?" the woman asked, not unkindly.

Eleanor hesitated. "No. Just passing through." The woman studied her a moment longer, then jerked her head toward a stump by the fire.

"Sit. You've the look of someone who hasn't eaten in days."

Eleanor sat.

The stew was hot and earthy, seasoned with wild herbs and root vegetables. Eleanor ate slowly, grateful for every bite.

"You're not from Taryn," the woman said, watching her. "Your voice is too clean. Too careful."

"I was born in Thaloria," Eleanor replied. "I'm... making my way to Wonderworth."

"Wonderworth?" the woman blinked. "That's a long ride yet. Especially on foot."

"I'll manage," Eleanor said.

The woman tilted her head. "Well, I've an old mare in the stable. Barely good for cart-pulling, but she still moves. You can have her—if you've something worth trading."

Eleanor reached into her satchel and withdrew one of the objects her mother had insisted she take: a small, jewelled brooch, shaped like a leaf, its edges traced in gold. It once belonged to her grandmother, she'd said. It wasn't much, but it glimmered faintly in the firelight.

The woman's eyes widened. "You sure?"

"I'm sure," Eleanor said, her throat tight.

The woman nodded solemnly and took the brooch. "You've got something weighing on you," she murmured. "I won't pry. But whatever it is... be careful. Wonderworth is not the kingdom it once was."

That night, Eleanor slept on a pile of hay in the cottage's loft. The woman—whose name was Brisa —didn't ask more questions. She offered warmth, bread, and silence. And in the morning, she handed Eleanor the reins to a grey-speckled mare named Della, along with a cloth-wrapped bundle of dried meat and boiled eggs.

Eleanor pressed her hand to her chest where the pendant lay. "Thank you."

Brisa simply nodded. "Ride swift. Stay true."

The road to Wonderworth was not paved. It was a fractured trail that twisted through shallow valleys and narrow mountain passes. Rain greeted her halfway through the second day, soaking her through her cloak. The cold returned with it, gnawing into her fingers and neck.

Della moved slowly, labouring over rocky terrain. Each step seemed harder for her, and Eleanor tried not to ask too much of the old mare. They camped by a stream, and Eleanor used her flint to spark a tiny fire beneath a rocky overhang. She fed the horse the last of the oats Brisa had packed and whispered to her like she used to whisper to her mother.

By the fourth day, Della's legs began to shake.

"No," Eleanor begged. "Just a little further, please."

But that night, the horse collapsed. Eleanor knelt beside her, stroking her flank until the creature stilled. Her fingers shook as she removed the bridle. The forest around her was silent, watching. She was alone again.

With blistered feet and aching limbs, Eleanor walked.

Each mile stretched endlessly. Her thoughts drifted —to her mother, to the grave under the birch tree, to the firelight dancing on Brisa's wrinkled face. And to her father. To Wonderworth. To what might await her when she arrived.

When she slept, it was in ditches and beneath trees, her cloak wrapped tight against the chill.

She dreamed of Zara—her soft voice, her strong will, the way she had hidden so much for so long. Eleanor could almost hear her mother humming the lullaby from her childhood, the one she used to sing under her breath when folding linens.

*Storm-born girl, the wind is your kin.*
*Run through the dark 'til the dawn lets you in.*

On the morning of the sixth day, Eleanor crested a rocky rise—and stopped dead in her tracks.

There it was.
Wonderworth Castle.

In the distance, past rolling golden hills and the sparkling curve of the River Malor, the castle stood like a dream. Its towers pierced the sky like pale fingers, the banners on its ramparts fluttering in the breeze. Sprawling fields and small villages dotted the land around it, and sunlight glinted off its high glass windows.

She sank to her knees.

Tears streamed down her cheeks—not only from relief but from the ache in her heart. This was the place her mother had once called home. The place Zara had fled. The place she had
sacrificed everything to keep Eleanor safe from.

How many nights had Zara cried alone in that little cottage, dreaming of this skyline? How many times had she looked at her daughter and ached for the life they could never claim?

"I'm here," Eleanor whispered through trembling lips. "Mama... I made it."

She stayed there for a long while, the wind curling through her hair, the scent of wildflowers on the air. Her bones ached. Her body was broken. But she had crossed the impossible.

The Outlands had not taken her.

The road had not broken her.
And Wonderworth—
Her future—
Now stood ahead.

# CHAPTER 3 - WHISPERS OF THE COURT

The towers of Wonderworth had seemed so distant from the ridge—but now, standing at its gates, Eleanor felt smaller than ever. Her cloak clung damp and heavy around her ankles, mud streaked her boots, and her legs trembled with fatigue. Days of walking had left her drained, but the castle loomed above her like a promise—one she'd bled for, one her mother had died for.

A pale carriage rattled out through the iron portcullis as Eleanor approached on foot, the cold morning wind tugging at her hood. Two guards in silver-and-black livery stood at attention. Their breastplates shone, but their expressions were dull with routine.

She paused before them, gathering what little strength she had left.

"Please," she said, voice cracked with weariness. "My name is Eleanor Labrelle. Daughter of Zara the Exiled. I seek audience with the king."

The guards exchanged a glance. One raised an eyebrow, the other sneered.

"Another beggar with a fantasy," the taller one muttered. "Go home, girl. Court's closed to wild stories."

"I have proof," Eleanor insisted, pulling the pendant from beneath her cloak. The silver glinted in the morning light—the crest of Wonderworth, unmistakable.

The shorter guard shifted uncomfortably, but his companion scoffed. "Pretty trinket. Plenty of fakes in the markets these days. King Edgar doesn't open his gates for the lost and filthy."

"I have come through the Outlands," she said. "I have crossed Taryn alone. I—" Her voice caught. "I am not here to beg. I claim my birthright."

"Then go around to the front gate," the tall guard said, unimpressed. "Or better yet, go home."

He turned away, indifferent.

Eleanor stood frozen, despair tightening around her throat. Her knees nearly buckled as she stepped back onto the stone path. People passed her—nobles in carriages, couriers, servants carrying linens and baskets of food. No one stopped. No one looked.

Until one did.

A weathered woman with a basket of towels paused, her sharp eyes scanning Eleanor's face. She blinked once—twice.

"You look like her," the woman said softly.

Eleanor turned, startled. "Like who?"

The woman stepped closer, lowering her voice. "Zara Labrelle. I remember her. We scrubbed floors in the east wing together, once. She had the same eyes as you—eyes that watched everything."

Eleanor's breath caught. "You knew her?"

The woman nodded. "She vanished when the queen mother's shadow stretched too far. We thought she'd died. But you—you're her echo."

"I need to see the steward," Eleanor whispered. "They won't let me in."

The woman looked both ways, then leaned in. "Follow me. There's a side door through the servant's hall. I'll see you brought in properly."

She led Eleanor around the side of the castle, through a narrow passage behind the kitchens. Inside, warmth wrapped around her like a forgotten dream. The housekeeper guided her to a small chamber where a washbasin waited. She helped Eleanor bathe, comb her tangled hair, and dress in a soft blue robe meant for a visiting attendant.

"You can't meet the king looking like you've been through hell," the woman said gently, patting her dry. "Even if you have."

Soon after, a page arrived with breathless urgency: "By order of King Edgar, Eleanor Labrelle is to present herself before His Majesty immediately."

Eleanor's heart galloped as she followed the page through arched corridors and marble halls lit by towering stained-glass windows. Her footsteps echoed on polished stone.

Finally, she reached the throne room.

The doors opened with a groan of iron and age. Sunlight streamed through high windows, casting long shadows across the tiled floor. At the far end, the dais stood beneath banners of silver and black. There, upon the throne, sat King Edgar—his figure stooped with time, curls silvered, a fur-lined mantle draped across his shoulders.

At his side stood Queen Thanamalice, tall and poised, her dark gown a column of cold elegance. Her expression was unreadable.

Eleanor bowed deeply, her voice trembling. "Your Majesty, I..."

King Edgar rose before she could finish. He descended the steps slowly, his hands trembling—not with weakness, but with emotion.

"Eleanor..." he said, his voice a broken prayer. "It cannot be. I was told—Zara... I thought she..."

"She lived," Eleanor said. "She raised me far from here. She died only days ago. Her final wish was that I find you."

The king came closer, searching her face. "You have her eyes," he whispered. "And her strength. She never once spoke of a child. They told me—my mother told me—"

"She said Zara bore no heir?" Eleanor asked gently.

He nodded, tears brimming in his eyes. "She lied. I see now. I see it all too late."

He stepped forward, arms wide. Eleanor hesitated —then rushed into his embrace. The weight of years crumbled in that moment. They wept together, for time lost, for love buried, for the life they might have known.

"I wanted to come for her," Edgar said into her hair. "But my mother… Morwenna… she exiled Zara under threat of death. I was made to marry. I could do nothing."

Eleanor pulled back, her face tear-streaked. "I understand now. She left so I might live. She never blamed you."

The king cupped her face with trembling hands. "You are my daughter. And you have returned to me."

From the dais, Thanamalice's gaze did not waver. Her expression cracked, just for a second regret? Guilt? Or calculation? —before her features smoothed once more.

She offered a single nod, then stepped forward. "Perhaps it is true. But time will tell."

As Eleanor stepped aside to let the king compose himself, whispers began to stir in the corners of the court. Pages hurried downside corridors. Courtiers glanced up from their scrolls. A messenger leaned toward a scribe and whispered, "The exiled girl lives." Another muttered, "That makes her next in line, doesn't it?"

Even from across the room, Eleanor felt the weight of every gaze that settled on her.

A steward bowed and quietly addressed the king.

"There are those who would contest her arrival, sire. Lords who swore loyalty to the queen's line will not be pleased."

Queen Thanamalice stepped forward again, her voice smooth as polished glass. "Blood may run true, but loyalty must be earned. If this girl is to stay, the court must see her proven. She cannot simply... appear and expect a crown."

Eleanor met her gaze and did not flinch. "I seek no crown. Only my place beside my father."

Thanamalice smiled without warmth. "Then you will have no objections to proving your claim."

The king's jaw tensed. "Enough. She will remain in the palace. She is my daughter, and I will not lose her again."

But Eleanor heard what went unspoken in the quiet glances exchanged behind velvet drapes and polished silver doors. Her return had stirred a court that fed on power. She was a threat—to some, a symbol of hope; to others, a danger waiting to unfold.

Her place here would not be given. It would have to be fought for.

And already, the court was sharpening its knives.

*\*\**

That night, long after the torches had dimmed and the castle had quieted to a hush, Eleanor found herself summoned to the old stone garden above the east tower—the one the servants still whispered was her mother's favorite spot.

She walked in silence, the hem of her gown brushing dew-slick grass, until she found him: King Edgar. Alone. Wrapped in a midnight cloak, seated on the low marble bench beneath the flowering ash tree, his eyes fixed on the stars above.

He looked older here. Smaller somehow. Just a man. Not a king.

"Eleanor," he said as she approached. "Come sit with me."

She joined him slowly, her hands folded in her lap.

For a long moment, neither of them spoke. The silence wasn't awkward. It was waiting.

Then he said softly, "You already know what happened between me and your mother."

Eleanor nodded. "She told me. Before she died."

His jaw tightened. "I never wanted to lose her. I fought for her—gods, I tried."

He leaned forward, elbows on his knees, voice thick with memory.

"She was just a servant in the palace when we met. New to court. She spilled wine on my tunic the first time we spoke. I should have been annoyed—but she was so sharp, so quick to speak her mind, and those eyes..."

He smiled faintly, lost in the past. "Your mother was brilliant. Not just beautiful—though she was that too—but clever. She saw the games everyone played, and she never bowed to them. I fell for her almost instantly."

He rubbed his palms together. "But she was a servant. I was a prince. We knew how dangerous it was. We met in secret, whispered in corridors, slipped notes into books in the library."

Eleanor watched him carefully. "What happened when your mother found out?"

His face shadowed. "Queen Morwenna—my mother —was a storm behind lace. Elegant and deadly. When she discovered the truth, she forbade me from ever seeing Zara again. Claimed it would ruin the kingdom. She moved Zara to the far kitchens, near the scullery, and threatened any servant who spoke to her without permission."

Eleanor's voice was quiet. "But you still found her."

"Of course I did," he whispered. "We risked everything. Every stolen moment was a rebellion. I didn't care about the throne. I only wanted her."

He closed his eyes. "But she never told me she was pregnant. If she had—gods, Eleanor—I would've defied everything. My mother, the crown, the council. I would have gone with her."

Eleanor's voice was barely a breath. "She didn't tell you because your mother found out first. She exiled her before she had the chance."

Edgar bowed his head, sadness overtook him.

"Queen Morwenna learned of the child—of me— and sent guards to have her removed before you ever knew."

For a heartbeat, the king was silent.


Then he crumbled.

Tears slipped down his weathered cheeks. He reached for her, and she met him halfway. They embraced tightly, years of silence and pain dissolving into the folds of royal velvet and trembling arms.

"I would've stopped it," he said into her hair. "I swear to the gods, I would've stopped it all. I would've chosen her. I never—never would've let her go."

Eleanor clutched him tighter. "She knew. And she never stopped loving you. Not once. She never hated you for what happened."

He sobbed softly, the king who ruled nations now nothing more than a man grieving for what he lost.

"Forgive me," he whispered. "Please, forgive me."

Eleanor pulled back, eyes shining. "There's nothing to forgive. You're here now. And I'm not leaving."

He brushed her hair behind her ear with trembling fingers. "Then I swear this before the gods and stars: I will never lose you again."


And in the silence that followed, under the branches of the ash tree that once sheltered a servant and a prince, a father and daughter became family at last.

# CHAPTER 4 - THE HALLS OF ICE

The summons arrived at dawn:
*By order of Queen Thanamalice, present yourself in His Majesty's solar at once.*

Eleanor stood in the corridor outside her chambers, the parchment trembling slightly in her hands. She had slept little—the walls of Wonderworth felt both familiar and foreign, like a dream she had once forgotten and now struggled to live inside.

She climbed the jade-carved staircase slowly, each step a reminder of where she had come from. Dirt still clung to her boots; her borrowed gown, though pressed and cleaned, still carried the scent of travel and earth.

The heavy oak doors stood before her, inlaid with lions and lilies—symbols of the old royal line. A final threshold between exile and something more.

Inside the chamber, sunlight filtered through latticed windows, casting intricate patterns on the polished stone floor. King Edgar stood at the window; his form bathed in pale gold.

At his side was Queen Thanamalice, draped in alabaster silk, her eyes cool and assessing. Her shoulders squared, chin lifted—with a raven-black braid looping down her back, and the high-collared bodice cinched at a narrow waist only to flare over hips laced in discreet corsetry. Every inch of her spoke of command, her lips a thin slash of red that never quite reached her calculating eyes.

Behind her stood Princess Nerezza, sharp-eyed and silent, arms crossed tightly over her chest. Her posture was impeccable—shoulders back, chin lifted—yet there was steel in the set of her lips and a calculating gleam in those emerald irises. Light caught the single braid looping over her shoulder, and the way her crimson-trimmed gown hugged her narrow waist only emphasized how every inch of her had been honed for both beauty and advantage.

"Eleanor," Edgar said, his voice soft but steady. "I present you to my wife and daughter."

Eleanor bowed. "Your Majesties."

Thanamalice did not bow in return. Her gaze moved from Eleanor's boots to the silver pendant at her neck. "She wears Zara's crest," the queen murmured, more to herself than anyone. "And claims Zara's blood."

"She is Zara's child," the king said, stepping closer. "And mine."

"Zara was banished," Thanamalice replied, still not looking at him. "My mother exiled her for scandal. I will not suffer scandal again."

Nerezza took a step forward, her voice like frost. "You have no place among us."

Eleanor kept her voice steady. "I came not to usurp, only to fulfil my mother's dying wish. To be known. To find my family."

Thanamalice's smile never touched her eyes. "Family must be earned, not claimed."

There was a long pause before Edgar stepped between them. "She will stay in the guest wing," he said. "She will dine with the court. She will not be hidden."

Thanamalice turned, her gown rustling like wind through ice. "As you wish, husband." Her words were formal, distant. "But do not ask me to welcome a reminder of what should have remained buried."

Nerezza followed her mother out, her expression unreadable—but not indifferent.

When they were gone, Edgar turned to Eleanor and took her hand. "You will face more subtle cruelty here than you did in the Outlands, my child. But you will not face it alone."

He brought her to a modest chamber in the guest wing—small but comfortable, with a proper bed, clean linens, and a window that overlooked the eastern garden. It was not a prison. It was not exile. But it was not acceptance either.

That evening, she dressed carefully in a gown that had been altered to fit her—a soft violet shade that brought colour to her cheeks. Her hair was braided in a simple twist. As she entered the grand hall, heads turned—not with ridicule, but with curiosity. Courtiers whispered, measured her, weighed her presence.

Eleanor did not flinch.

She was seated near the lower end of the long table—not beside the king but not banished to the shadows. A fair seat for someone not yet declared, but not entirely unwelcome. Servants brought her roasted fowl and warm bread, and though Nerezza barely glanced her way, several noblewomen offered polite nods. A scholar from the court bowed to her with quiet respect. It was not affection—but it was not contempt.

Still, beneath it all, she could feel the chill of Thanamalice's gaze from across the room. The queen's circle of loyal lords and ladies watched Eleanor with hawk's eyes, noting every word, every movement. Nerezza, too, whispered to a visiting nobleman—eyes never quite leaving Eleanor's face.

Later, as the feast waned, Eleanor slipped out into the moonlit corridor. The sound of laughter echoed through the halls—some bright, some forced. A pair of guards she passed nodded politely. A maid paused to curtsy; her eyes wide with wonder.

"Is it true, my lady?" the girl whispered. "That you came through the Outlands alone?"

Eleanor managed a small smile. "Yes."

The girl beamed; her awe genuine. "Then I hope you stay. The court needs someone brave."

Back in her chambers, Eleanor stood at the window and looked out across the gardens. Her mother had once walked these halls—hidden, watched, shamed. And now her daughter stood in her place.

She pressed the pendant to her lips.

"For Mother. For Father. For the truth."

The wind whispered across the grounds like a voice long silenced. Eleanor closed her eyes and knew - she was not just surviving. She was becoming.

# CHAPTER 5 -
# COURTLY GAMES AND
# HIDDEN FLAMES

The early morning sun streamed through the stained-glass windows of the east gallery, casting jewelled light across the marble floors as Eleanor descended the grand staircase. Now clad in lavender silk that hugged her hourglass curves, her hair swept up to frame a face of soft cheekbones and full lips, she carried herself with both the poise of a noblewoman and the fire of a born survivor. Her lavender gown moved softly behind her; her hair braided with delicate ribbon. She felt eyes on her—curious, cautious, speculative

—but not cruel. Since her arrival, the palace had become a place of measured tension rather than open hostility. Everyone was waiting to see what she would become.

At the foot of the stairs stood a stranger—tall, broad-shouldered, dressed in riding leathers marked with the sigil of Bravethorne. His thick, dark hair fell in careless waves around a strong brow; a neatly trimmed beard framed jaw muscles that hinted at both strength and weariness, and his forest-green eyes lingered on her with sober intensity. He was deep in quiet conversation with a steward, but something made him glance up just as Eleanor stepped into the light.

Their eyes met.

Prince Roman had returned to court that morning without ceremony, weary from a week of border inspections. He'd heard only whispers on his way in—mention of a mysterious woman who had appeared at Wonderworth and now occupied a guest chamber at the king's invitation. No one knew her true origin. No one dared to speak her name with certainty.

Until now, he had not believed the rumours worth a second thought.

But now she stood before him.

Graceful, composed, unfamiliar—and utterly captivating.

Roman stepped away from the steward, closing the space between them with quiet intent. "Good morning," he said, his voice low, warm. "I don't believe we've met."

Eleanor tilted her head, intrigued by his calm boldness. "No, we haven't."

"I'm Roman," he offered. "Bravethorne."

"I'm Eleanor," she said carefully, her eyes never leaving his.

Roman raised a brow. "So, it's true. You do exist."

She smiled faintly. "That's one way to begin a conversation."

"I heard the court speak of someone new. Mysterious. Brave. Dangerous, even. I assumed they were exaggerating." He studied her openly. "Now I'm not so sure."

Eleanor gave a short laugh. "And what do you make of me now?"

"I'm still deciding," he said honestly.

Before she could respond, a sharp voice cut across the corridor like a blade.
"Roman!"

Princess Nerezza swept into the corridor in a forest-green gown shot through with jet beading, the fabric whispering around her long, lithe frame. Dark curls crowned her head, offsetting skin so pale it seemed carved from marble—yet her green eyes burned with a fire that spoke of both wounded pride and ruthless intent. Her eyes locked on Eleanor with immediate disdain.

"There you are," she said coolly, glancing between them. "We have appointments, remember?"

Roman gave Eleanor a regretful look. "Duty calls. But I do hope we meet again."

"I'm not difficult to find," Eleanor said softly.

As Nerezza pulled him away by the arm, Eleanor stood in the flood of coloured light, her breath catching in her throat. Roman hadn't known who she was. That made his attention feel... real. Unfiltered by rumour or claim.

It made it dangerous, too.

\*\*\*

In the private gallery, Nerezza turned on Roman the moment they were alone.

"You can't talk to her," she hissed. "Do you even know who she is?"

"She said her name is Eleanor."

"She's the exile's daughter," Nerezza spat. "The

one my father claims as his blood. The one who threatens *everything*."

Roman's brows lifted. "The one whose name you've refused to speak?"

"The one whose name I *won't* let replace mine."

Before he could respond, the doors opened, and Queen Thanamalice swept in.

"You're both here. Good." Her voice was soft but iron-edged. "Have you chosen a date yet?"

Roman gave a short bow. "I would prefer to wait until the king is stronger."

"Wait too long," Thanamalice replied, "and you may not be prince long enough to matter."

She turned to her daughter. "Heirs must be secured. The banns will be read next moon's dawn."

Nerezza bowed. "Yes, Mother."

Roman said nothing. But his eyes drifted to the staircase where he had seen Eleanor, and something in his chest tightened.

\*\*\*

That night, Eleanor slipped quietly through the castle's side halls, her slippers soundless against the flagstones. She needed air. Space. A moment untouched by politics and judgment.

The moonlight bathed the gardens in silver. Aurelions bloomed beneath the stars, their petals opening in luminous sighs. Whispervine curled lazily across trellises, humming softly in the wind. The air was cool and damp with promise.

Eleanor found herself at the lilypool again. The water shimmered with reflections of stars—bright, infinite, impossibly close.

"Found you," said a voice.

She turned, startled—then eased. Roman.

He stood beneath the archway, hands at his sides, not approaching too quickly.

"I didn't mean to intrude," he said. "But I hoped we might talk. Properly, this time."

She folded her arms. "You've learned who I am, I take it?"

"I have," he said honestly. "And it changes nothing."

"It should," she whispered. "You're betrothed to a woman who hates me, and I—"

"You are a woman who fascinates me," he finished.

The silence that followed was full of things unsaid.

"You don't even know me," she said.

"I know what the court says. I know you crossed the Outlands alone. I know you speak with fire but walk softly. And I know... I would like to know more."

He stepped closer. She didn't move.

"May I?" he asked.

She nodded; not exactly knowing what he was going to do, breath caught in her throat.

The kiss was not rushed. It was thoughtful, slow— like reading the first page of a long story. Her heart hammered in her chest; every nerve alive. When they parted, their foreheads touched.

But then she stepped back. "You shouldn't have—"

Roman didn't protest. "I apologise."

Eleanor turned and fled beneath the trellis; her steps muffled by moss. She didn't stop until her turret door closed behind her.

*\*\**

She sat on her mattress until the sun rose.

Every moment replayed in her mind—the brush of his hand, the intensity of his eyes, the sheer clarity of *wanting* something for herself.

But there were consequences.

*\*\**

By midday, the court was whispering.

Lady Virelle had seen them walking too close in the gallery. A young squire had spotted Roman heading toward the gardens alone. One of Nerezza's handmaidens had noticed Eleanor's absence from her chambers for over an hour.

Nerezza stood at the top of the inner courtyard, lips pale with fury.

Thanamalice noticed. *Like mother, like daughter.*

"Be patient, daughter," the queen said coolly. "Let the girl make her mistakes. She will be judged for them. Not by us—but by everyone watching."

Nerezza's eyes burned. "She's already begun."

\*\*\*

Eleanor remained in her chambers most of the day. The castle that had once been curious now felt dangerous, its corridors echoing with judgment even in silence.

The kiss had been innocent—yet it burned on her lips like wildfire. She pressed her fingers there, heat lingering against her skin and memory. She had wanted it, craved it, and that scared her more than anything. Her heart thundered at the thought of Roman's rough beard brushing hers, his green eyes alight with something fierce and hungry.

But alongside that rush came guilt, bitter as gall. She pictured Lady Nerezza's proud tilt of the chin, the unspoken promise she had made to a friend and ally. Eleanor's pulse stuttered with shame: how could she betray one woman's trust for another's touch?

A storm raged through her mind—her duty whispering one way, her desire roaring another. Reason tugged at her sleeve, reminding her of the dangers of passion in court; emotion pulled her into Roman's orbit once more.

She clenched her fists, knuckles white. She didn't regret it. Not yet. But already she wondered: whose side would win this war within her heart?

# CHAPTER 5.5 - THE
# SPACE BETWEEN
# FIRE AND FOG

E leanor did not see Roman again for three days.

Not because he avoided her, but because the court itself closed around her like a tightening corset. Every waking hour was filled with etiquette drills, council introductions, and interviews with curious nobles whose interest ranged from subtle admiration to thinly veiled suspicion. The queen had ensured that Eleanor's schedule was packed tight, and while Thanamalice offered no overt hostility, the effect was the same as exile: isolation by ritual.

Meanwhile, in the north, the kingdom of Isendra teetered on the brink of full rebellion. A splinter faction calling itself the Dawnbringers declared open defiance of the royal line, taking control of several border towns and cutting off trade to Wonderworth. Messengers came and went from the war room, cloaked in urgency. Whispers of battle-ready allies and secret envoys drifted through the halls. Lord Varn of the eastern marches began petitioning for more garrison funding— ostensibly to defend Wonderworth, but everyone knew he was angling for power in the wake of King Edgar's decline.

In the west, Taryn deployed naval scouts along the shared coast with Silverhaven. Skirmishes on the sea were being downplayed, but the merchant guilds whispered of a trade war brewing. The balance of power was shifting. Each kingdom tested its neighbours with subtler blades than swords.

Eleanor bore her burdens with measured grace, answering questions about her upbringing, her education, even her favourite teas—all while watching the shadows of the court shift around her. A few lords tested her poise with double-edged compliments. A few ladies offered friendship with the warmth of a snake basking in sunlight. And through it all, Eleanor kept her spine straight and her tongue sharp but controlled.

Roman, for his part, kept his distance—but not his eyes. More than once, Eleanor caught him watching her from across the feasting hall, from the stables, from the upper gallery above the council chambers. He always looked away first. But she felt the weight of his gaze each time, and she was sure he knew it.

One morning, during an emergency council meeting about Isendra, Eleanor stood by the map table, observing silently as lords argued over border defences and tribute cuts. She remembered the lessons her mother had quietly shared—how Zara, once confined to the edges of royal corridors, had overheard Edgar and his father discuss statecraft for hours. Zara, sharp and observant, had absorbed every word and later passed that knowledge to her daughter during evenings by the fire. Eleanor knew the structure of trade routes, the subtleties of alliance negotiations, and the vulnerabilities of royal pride.

Lord Carren fumed over grain supplies being intercepted. Lord Verrick proposed closing the eastern routes entirely.

Eleanor, ignored until then, stepped forward.

"What if we diverted merchant routes west, through the lower hills of Bravethorne? The terrain is rougher, but fewer eyes are on it. Smugglers already use it."

The room fell silent.

Lord Verrick scoffed. "That's bandit territory."

"Yes," she said coolly, "which is why no one would expect a royal-sanctioned convoy to go through it. With discreet escort and staggered timing, we could maintain supply lines and avoid open conflict."

Roman stared at her, blinking.

King Edgar, frail but attentive, gave a soft nod. "Write it up. We'll present it to the trade envoy at dusk."

Later, outside the chamber, Roman caught up to her.

"I didn't expect you to speak," he said.

"I didn't expect anyone to listen," she replied.

He smiled slowly. "They did. I did. That was brilliant."

His voice held something deeper now—admiration threaded through curiosity, laced with the danger of wanting someone for more than just beauty.

Back in the capital of Taryn, Duke Aldric's fury boiled. His son's name now swirled through the scandal-ridden letters from Wonderworth. Marriage negotiations hung by a thread. He dispatched Lady Coren with orders: find out if the rumours of Roman's infatuation were true, and if they were, crush them.

Eleanor's next meeting with Roman took place in the armoury courtyard. She had gone there to breathe, to escape the endless eyes. Roman had come to drill.

She watched him spar with two guards, swift and relentless. When he noticed her, he smiled despite his breathlessness.

"I didn't think politics and steel mixed," she teased.

"Sometimes, swords make better points than words," he said.

She stepped onto the sand, picked up a practice blade.

"Care to test that?"

Their bout was short, but it ended with Eleanor knocking the sword from his hand. Roman laughed as he retrieved it.

"You're full of surprises."

"So are you," she said.

A shadow passed over them—Nerezza. Her voice cut the air.

"Perhaps the court should host a tourney. I'm sure the exile would enjoy a more public duel."

Eleanor lowered her sword, spine straight. "If they let exiles fight, I imagine we'd win."

That night, Roman found her in the east gallery.

"I want to know everything," he said. "What you've read. What you see when you look at this kingdom. How you think."

"And if it challenges what you believe?" she asked.

"I hope it does."

They spoke until the candles burned low.

When he took her hand this time, she didn't pull away.

Their fingers twined, and though they didn't kiss, the closeness between them had shifted—no longer a question, but a slow, undeniable answer.

In the shadows of the royal war room, Lord Verrick and two advisors discussed Isendra's instability.

"If the Dawnbringers succeed, they'll seek legitimacy. And who better to challenge Wonderworth's rule than a girl born from scandal?"

"You mean to align with rebels?" asked the steward.

"I mean to survive whatever storm this court refuses to name."

By the fifth meeting, Eleanor and Roman had stopped pretending to be surprised.

They found each other beneath the western arbour where the court rarely walked. Roman brought wine and figs. Eleanor brought silence and a hunger she wouldn't name.

They didn't kiss.
Not yet.

But they sat with their knees touching. And when a warm breeze rustled the canopy above, Roman whispered, "When the storm comes, I want you beside me."
Eleanor looked up at him, eyes wide. "And when it passes?"

He didn't answer.
Because he didn't know.
Before they could say more, footsteps approached. One of Nerezza's handmaids emerged from the shadows, clearly sent to interrupt.
"My lord," she said, "Princess Nerezza requests your presence in the east salon. Urgently."
Roman rose reluctantly, gaze still fixed on Eleanor.
"Until next time," he said.
And the ache of not saying more lingered long after

he was gone.

That night, they dreamed of each other.
And the dreams felt real.

Beyond the walls of the palace, the kingdom whispered. And not all those whispers were in favour of the crown.

# CHAPTER 6 - THE QUEEN'S WELCOME BALL

**W**eeks passed, but the memory of that moonlit kiss never left Eleanor.

She had seen Roman only from a distance since. A nod across the council courtyard. A glance too brief to carry meaning. Nerezza clung closer to him than ever, as though daring the court to speak of what she suspected. And the court—*oh, the court*—had grown thick with whispers.

But it was not the kiss that dominated conversation now. It was the ball.

Wonderworth prepared itself with the urgency of a kingdom trying to rewrite its story in lace and gold. In the sunlit courtyard, artisans erected archways draped in silver ribbons and dawnlight roses, petals that shimmered by day and glowed by night. Musicians rehearsed endlessly in the high galleries. Servants rushed with bolts of silk and trays of crystal goblets. The air itself seemed charged with expectation.

Even in distant kingdoms, nobles whispered of it—Silverhaven, Taryn, even Thaloria. A royal daughter, long lost, now returned. And tonight, she would stand before them all.

Inside Eleanor's chamber, the scent of polished wood and lavender filled the air. Attendants moved quietly, pinning pale blue silk at her shoulders, adjusting her bodice, sliding pearl combs into her hair. In the mirror, Eleanor hardly recognized herself.

"You are Wonderworth's moon tonight, my lady," one of the maids whispered.

At the appointed hour, the clang of a ceremonial gong echoed through the terrace and halls. Jasper the Herald, auburn-haired and sharp in vibrant livery, stepped onto the marble dais with a scroll in hand.

The court fell silent.

"People of Wonderworth," he proclaimed, voice clear beneath the evening stars, "by royal decree of His Majesty King Edgar the Third, we welcome Lady Eleanor Labrelle—long hidden, now returned—to her rightful place as heir to the crown."

Gasps and murmurs swept through the gathering. All eyes turned.

At the top of the grand staircase, Eleanor stood poised, luminous in pale silk that caught the firelight like moon-glow. Her mother's pendant rested against her breast. She descended slowly, each step measured, graceful—royal.

From a high balcony, Queen Thanamalice observed in silence, lips unreadable. Princess Nerezza loomed nearby, arms folded, jaw tight.

At the foot of the stairs, King Edgar waited. His eyes brimmed with tears as he reached for Eleanor's hands.

"My child," he whispered, voice cracking, "you are

truly here."

Eleanor leaned forward, embracing him. "I have come home, Father."

He drew back to study her. "You endured so much. From the birch cottage to the Outlands... what pain, what strength."

"Mother taught me well," she said. "Her spirit walks with me tonight."

Edgar's tears fell freely as he kissed her brow. "Tonight, you shine brighter than any court jewel. I am proud to call you my daughter."

They turned to face the court. For the first time in decades, father and daughter stood together beneath Wonderworth's banners.


Then came the music.

A slow, expectant chord unfurled from the orchestra. From the shadows stepped Prince Roman, clad in deep green velvet, his eyes locked on Eleanor as he approached the dais.

The murmurs began again—soft, stunned.


Before he could speak, Nerezza appeared from the side corridor, voice sharp. "Roman! How dare you present yourself to a stranger when your betrothed awaits?"

He paused mid-step. "Engagement matters can wait. Tonight, I honour the king's heir first."

"Do not forget your responsibilities!" she snapped. "Mother expects us at Aurelius Keep by moonrise. I will not be overshadowed."

She spun and disappeared into the crowd.

Roman turned back to Eleanor. "Lady Eleanor," he said with warmth and intent, "may I have this dance?"

Her breath caught. She nodded and placed her hand in his.

The music swelled, and together they stepped into the candlelit terrace.

They moved with perfect rhythm—unpracticed, yet effortless. Around them, nobles watched in silence, uncertain whether to envy, admire, or condemn.

Roman's hand rested lightly at her waist, his other guiding hers as they turned beneath the stars. Eleanor's heart pounded, not from fear—but from *freedom.* For the first time since her arrival, she felt seen not as a symbol, but as a woman.

"You are radiant," he whispered as the final chord faded.

They lingered in stillness, then slipped away from

the crowd. Down marble halls, through rose-scented galleries, and out into a private garden where lanterns floated like fireflies above arching jasmine vines.

As they entered a secluded tent draped in ivory silks, Eleanor turned to him, cheeks flushed, breath shallow.

Roman touched her cheek, reverently. "You are not what I expected," he murmured. "You are so much more."

She swallowed hard. "You'll be expected to marry her. Nerezza."

"I am expected to do many things," he said. "But what I *choose*—that is mine."

His lips met hers again, deeper this time. No pretence. No performance.

His hands slid through her hair, down the arch of her back, pressing her gently against the soft cushions beneath the canopy. Her fingers clutched at his sleeves as he kissed down her throat, his breath warm, his touch sure. He parted her bodice with reverent slowness, as if unwrapping something sacred.

"Are you certain?" he asked, voice barely a whisper.

Eleanor nodded, breath catching. "I want this. I want *you*."

They moved together—soft sighs, stolen touches, hearts laid bare. The court, the crown, the expectations—they all faded into the hush of jasmine and stars. Here, they were only man and woman. Desire. Trust. Fire.

Later, tangled in silken sheets and the afterglow of wonder, Roman held her close. She lay with her head on his chest, listening to the beat of something new and undeniable.

"This night is ours," he murmured.

And Eleanor, eyes closed, whispered, "Let it be the first of many."

Afterglow.

Later, when Roman had fallen asleep beside her, Eleanor lay awake beneath the veil of silken drapes, her body still tingling with the memory of his touch. The jasmine-scented night wrapped around her like a dream, but her mind would not quiet.

She had never known such closeness. Not just the physicality of it—though every part of her still burned with the imprint of his hands—

but the *vulnerability* it demanded. He had kissed her with fire, touched her like she mattered, and in return, she had given him everything. Freely. Willingly.

And now, she didn't know what to do with the storm inside her.

She turned slightly on the cushions, pulling the satin sheet around her bare shoulders. Her heart fluttered—not from fear, but something like awe. *So, this is what it feels like.* To be desired. To be seen. To let down every wall and not be cast aside.

She touched her lips gently, still swollen from his. Her body ached in unfamiliar ways, not with pain, but with *change*. She had stepped through a doorway tonight, and there would be no turning back.

*I gave myself to him,* she thought. *And I wanted to.*

A small smile curved her lips. That truth was pure. She did not regret it.

But beneath the warmth coiled another feeling. A knot of worry pulling tight in her chest.

*He is betrothed to Nerezza.*

The thought struck cold. She sat up slowly, drawing the blanket higher. The silk felt delicate against her skin, but no softer than the moment she had stolen—borrowed, perhaps—from another woman's future.

Nerezza, who loathed her. Nerezza, who held the queen's favour. Nerezza, who had watched her descend the staircase tonight with fury in her eyes.

*What have I done?*

For a brief, wild moment, Eleanor had let herself believe she was just a woman in love, and not the daughter of a disgraced exile entangled in court politics. But she wasn't free. Roman wasn't free.

And yet... he had chosen her.

She closed her eyes, placing a hand over her heart.

She had always wondered what it might feel like —to be touched, held, cherished. But she'd never imagined how *complicated* it would be when it finally happened. This wasn't some secret, perfect thing tucked away in a cottage. This was the palace. The court. A kingdom on edge. And the man she had given herself to belonged to someone else—at least in the eyes of the world.

*Will he still look at me tomorrow? Or will he pretend this never happened?*

Her thoughts tangled like threads, torn between joy and shame, longing and fear.

Still, a voice echoed inside her—quiet, certain, and shaped like her mother's:

*You are not a mistake. You are not his secret. You are enough.*

Tears welled in her eyes, not from regret, but from the weight of becoming. She was not the same girl who crossed the River Orwain. Not the frightened daughter burying her mother in the birch grove. She had stepped into power. Into womanhood.

Into herself.

And though the world might rage come morning, for now, in this hidden corner of the royal garden, she allowed herself the rarest of luxuries:

Hope.

The lanterns still flickered above the jasmine archways, but Eleanor was gone.

Roman stood alone now beneath the canopy of

ivory silk, the scent of her still clinging to the cushions, the warmth of her body fading from the place where they'd lain. A breath ago, she'd been in his arms.

Now, only silence remained. And yet the garden pulsed with everything that had passed between them.

He ran a hand through his hair, the other tightening into a fist. The night had changed him —undone something careful and rehearsed. He felt like he'd stepped off a ledge with no idea where the ground was. All he knew was the feeling of her fingers clutching his sleeves, the way her breath had hitched when he touched her, the fire in her voice when she said I want you.

Gods help him, he wanted her too.

Wanted her still.

But desire was the easy part.

He stepped into the moonlight, staring up at the stars as if they might offer a verdict. His pulse still hadn't settled. His mind wouldn't quiet. The truth cut sharp and clean: he had crossed a line tonight. Not just as a prince. As a man promised to someone else.

To Nerezza.

His mouth twisted at the name. Betrothal, duty, alliance—it all sounded noble in theory. But in practice, it felt like a shackle.

Nerezza didn't love him. She wanted the crown, the power, the control. She had never once looked at him the way Eleanor had in the shadows of this garden—like he was more than a title. More than leverage.

Roman sat on the edge of the fountain, elbows on his knees, fingers threading together. Water trickled beside him, soft and steady, a cruel contrast to the storm inside his chest. What was he supposed to do now? What if tonight was a mistake? No. He shook his head. That wasn't true. It hadn't been a mistake. It had been real. More real than anything he'd known in the hollow pageantry of courtship and obligation. Eleanor had seen him —truly seen him. And for once, he hadn't flinched from being known. But reality waited just beyond the garden walls.

The court would talk. The Queen would rage. Nerezza—gods, she would make him bleed for this. She'd use her fury like a dagger and twist it in public and private alike. She would not go quietly. She would not go without dragging Eleanor's name through the dirt. And that was what terrified him most—not for himself, but for Eleanor.

What if he had ruined her? What if his need, his rebellion, his desire had pulled her into a war she never asked for? He closed his eyes, pressing the heels of his palms to his brow. He didn't know how to protect her now. Not without betraying everything he'd been raised to uphold. Not without setting fire to every alliance the kingdom had balanced itself upon. And yet...

She had not run from him. She had walked into the night with her head held high, even after all they'd shared. She was brave. Braver than him.

Roman exhaled slowly. The garden no longer felt like a refuge. It felt like a moment borrowed from a life that didn't belong to him. A sanctuary about to be breached. Still, he clung to it. To her. To the memory of her lips, her voice, her choice. Maybe he didn't have a plan yet. Maybe he didn't know how to fix what came next. But he knew this: he wouldn't let her become a casualty of his cowardice. Not this time.

He rose, casting one last look toward the path she had taken. The jasmine vines swayed gently, as if still whispering her name.

Tomorrow would be war. But tonight—tonight was theirs.

# CHAPTER 7 - RUMOURS
# AT DAWN

The knock came before sunrise.

Three sharp raps against the wooden door of Eleanor's turret chamber—firm, practiced, not servant's hands.

Eleanor jolted awake, heart pounding, the soft sheets tangled around her legs. For a moment she forgot where she was, still half-dreaming of jasmine-scented nights and the weight of Roman's hand in hers.

Then she remembered. The ball. The dance. The

kiss. The tent.

Her cheeks burned as she sat up, brushing curls from her face. Her shift was wrinkled, her body still aching in a way she couldn't name without blushing.

The knock came again.

"My lady," a voice called through the door—Anaïs, the queen's lady-in-waiting. "The queen summons you. Now."

Eleanor's pulse skipped. "The queen?"

"She expects you in her solar within the quarter bell. Wear something appropriate."

The footsteps retreated before Eleanor could answer. She exhaled slowly, steadying her breath. *This is it,* she thought. The mood had changed.

She dressed quickly in a muted grey gown, cinching it tightly around her waist. No pearls, no ribbons, no dawnlight silk. She braided her hair plainly, washed her face, and pressed a kiss to her mother's pendant before stepping out.

The halls were quiet, but not empty.

Servants passed her without speaking. One bowed with a stiff neck, not quite meeting her eyes. Two courtiers glanced up from a conversation and fell abruptly silent as she approached. Whispers chased her steps like smoke.

By the time she reached the queen's solar, her stomach was twisted in knots.

The doors stood open. Inside, Queen Thanamalice sat beneath an arched window, pouring tea into a delicate porcelain cup. She did not look up.

"Enter," she said simply.

Eleanor stepped inside and stood tall, refusing to shrink beneath the chill in the air.

Thanamalice stirred honey into her tea and set the spoon aside with delicate precision. Then she lifted her gaze.

"You danced well last night," she said, voice calm. "A fitting performance for the daughter of a once-removed servant."

Eleanor said nothing. The queen's eyes glittered—sharp, dark, cold.

"But it was not the dancing that disturbed the court," she continued. "It was the closeness. The *lingering*. The whispers it fed."

Eleanor's fingers curled at her sides. "We shared a

dance. Nothing more."

"Did you?" Thanamalice's voice never rose. "You forget how closely people watch a royal heir, especially one whose claim is so... recent."

A pause.

"I am not here to scold you," she went on. "But to remind you—*visibly*—that we live in a palace, not a dream. Prince Roman is promised to my daughter. Your actions, whether innocent or not, reflect on the crown."

Eleanor met her gaze evenly. "I acted with dignity. If others imagined more, that is their failing, not mine." Eleanor surprised herself. Was she trying to convince herself or the Queen?

Thanamalice studied her a moment longer. Then she smiled—thin and dangerous. "We shall see if that poise survives court life."

She gestured toward the door. "That will be all, Lady Eleanor. You are expected at the morning council. Do not be late."

***

Eleanor exited into the corridor with a straight spine, but her mind swirled.

She didn't make it far before a figure stepped out

from a side passage.

Nerezza.

Clad in a forest green gown with jet beading, she looked as though she had slept in her fury. Her eyes locked on Eleanor like daggers drawn.

"You have gall," she said quietly. "Dancing with *my* betrothed beneath the stars, like some fairy-tale enchantress."

Eleanor didn't flinch. "It was one dance."

Nerezza took a step forward. "You're not the first to beguile a man with wounded eyes and tragic stories. But I *am* the one with power."

"You're the one clinging to a man who looks elsewhere," Eleanor said evenly. Her heart skipping a beat at her own audacity.

Nerezza's jaw tightened. "He pities you. That's all."

"If that helps you sleep, then believe it." And again.

A long, brittle silence passed between them.

Then Nerezza leaned closer, voice like ice cracking over a frozen lake. "This place may welcome you now. But it only takes one misstep for a house of cards to fall. I'll be waiting."

She swept away without another word.

Eleanor released a breath she hadn't realized she was holding. Her hands trembled, but her chin remained high.

The first battle had begun—and it would not be the last.

\*\*\*

The sun had barely crested the hills when Eleanor arrived at the council chamber. The great oak doors stood open, revealing a long table surrounded by nobles, advisors, and stewards in hushed conversation. The king's standard hung limp in the still air, flanked by the House of Wonderworth's silver lions and black banners.

Eleanor entered, drawing glances—some polite, some wary. She was no longer invisible, but not yet embraced. She had walked into the belly of the kingdom's power, and already the air felt colder.

King Edgar sat slumped at the head of the table, eyes tired, his once-sturdy frame diminished beneath layers of furs. He offered Eleanor a faint smile as she bowed. "Come, child. Stand beside me."

She did.

To his left sat Lord Hawthorne, the realm's master of ships. To his right, an empty chair. Thanamalice's.

The queen had not come.

Instead, her voice lingered in the whispers between lords: *The girl danced with the Bravethorne heir. The king looked frail last night. A shift is coming.*

Eleanor stood tall and silent, listening as trade routes were discussed, border tensions with Taryn reviewed. But her thoughts were far from the parchments and seal-rings on the table.

She couldn't shake the sense that something deeper had begun to unfold.

***

Elsewhere in the palace…

Morning light crept through the mullioned windows of the queen's solar, gilding its velvet drapes in quiet gold. But there was nothing soft in the room's mood.

Princess Nerezza burst in, her fury barely held by poise.

"He danced with *her*," she seethed. "And then disappeared into the gardens! I waited for him, and he never came. Everyone saw it, Mother—everyone. I think he's—"

"Fallen for the upstart," Queen Thanamalice finished, her voice smooth as poured cream. She did

WHERE THE CROWN FELL

not rise from her divan but continued arranging folds of silk over the lounge as if she were dressing a corpse.

Nerezza's fists curled. "I demanded Father move our union forward. If Roman refuses me, what becomes of our alliance?"

Thanamalice finally looked up, her face as still as sculpture. "You forget yourself. This kingdom does not run on affection—it runs on obedience. And your father's time to rule it has long since passed."

Nerezza blinked. "You mean—"

"I mean," Thanamalice interrupted, rising slowly, "that I have no patience for dithering kings who let exile daughters play heiress." She stood at full height—tall, statuesque—her alabaster-white silk gown falling in precise folds to the marble floor. Jet-black hair was swept into a severe knot at her nape, framing cheekbones sharp enough to cast half-shadows, and her pale, storm-grey eyes held the court in unblinking appraisal.

She crossed to the window, gazing out over the eastern gardens.

"He was once a man of vision," she said distantly. "Now he's little more than a wheezing relic propped up by sentiment."

Her voice sharpened. "If he won't abdicate, nature will do what he refuses."

Nerezza's face paled. "You mean to—"

"Secure your future," Thanamalice said smoothly, turning to her daughter. "That is all I ever mean."

"But how—"

"Leave it to me."

She placed a hand gently on Nerezza's shoulder. "Play your part. Be sweet. Be silent. Let the court see the dutiful daughter. And tonight—leave the rest to me."

***

When Nerezza was gone, Queen Thanamalice moved alone through her private chamber, silent as a shadow. She opened a concealed drawer and removed a small crystal vial, plum-hued and clear. No label. No scent.

She carried it to the sideboard and poured the contents—just a single drop—into the ornate silver decanter reserved for the king's evening wine. The liquid swirled, then vanished.

By the lantern-light, her smooth ivory skin gleamed nearly as brightly as the silver filigree on her sleeves; every movement was measured, from the taper-straight back of her neck to the slight curl of her crimson-stained lips—beauty wielded like a blade.

"No trace," she whispered to herself. "No suspicion."

The glass caught her reflection: regal, composed, merciless.

"If you are not man enough to finish your reign," she said to the empty air, "I will finish it for you."

\*\*\*

Back in the council chamber, King Edgar coughed harshly, waving away a steward's offered cup. "I'm fine," he wheezed.

Eleanor stepped toward him instinctively. "Let me —"

"No," he whispered, eyes locking with hers. "They mustn't see."

He smiled faintly again. "Too many eyes. Too many wolves."

Eleanor squeezed his hand beneath the table. "Then we stand as lions."

Edgar's eyes glistened—not with tears, but pride. "My daughter," he murmured, "you are the future."

Eleanor looked up and caught the narrowed gaze of Lord Verrick, one of the queen's staunchest allies.

He was already whispering to the steward beside him. Something was stirring in the court.

And she would need to be ready for it.

# CHAPTER 8 -
# CAPTIVE PATHS

The castle grew colder as King Edgar's health faded—first in his steps, then in his voice, and finally in the way no one said his name above a whisper anymore.

Servants moved quieter now. Courtiers lingered less around his chambers. And Eleanor felt it in her bones—like frost creeping down palace walls. The kingdom was bracing for a power shift. And not all would welcome her when it came.

The morning after the council, she found her father's seat empty. The excuse given was fatigue. But no one looked surprised. Not even the steward.

Not even the guards outside his door.

Whispers spread like oil across marble:
*"The king's cups sit untouched."*
*"He coughed blood last night."*
*"He's stopped signing documents."*
*"Soon, she will rule alone."*

*She.* Thanamalice.

***

That afternoon, Eleanor was summoned to the queen's solar.

The room was as beautiful as ever—tapestries in sunset hues, furniture lacquered to gleam like obsidian—but it smelled too strongly of perfume, like something dead had been covered in roses.

Queen Thanamalice sat at her writing desk, a glass of dark wine at her elbow. Her smile was gracious, her eyes cold.

"Lady Eleanor," she began, voice like velvet over iron. "Your presence has stirred the halls, and not just for the worse. Several noble houses have expressed interest in... forming ties."

Eleanor's throat tightened. "You mean marriage proposals."

"Private suitor visits," the queen confirmed. "A

chance to broaden your understanding of court life. And to reframe certain… distractions." Her gaze, sharp and deliberate, flicked toward the garden beyond the window—where Roman had danced with Eleanor under starlight just days ago.

Eleanor stiffened. "Must I accept them all?"

"You will *entertain* them," Thanamalice said smoothly, rising from her chair. "You may even impress one. Imagine, a future secured with silk and silence. Isn't that what your mother would've wanted?"

Eleanor met her gaze. "My mother wanted me free."

Thanamalice's smile tightened. "Then let's start with choosing your cage."

***

As Eleanor stepped out, shaken but proud, she nearly collided with Anaïs, the queen's lady-in-waiting.

"Careful, my lady," Anaïs murmured, steadying her. She glanced around, then leaned in. "Some of these men the queen's inviting… they don't want wives. They want leverage."

Eleanor searched her face. "Why warn me?"

Anaïs shrugged. "Not everyone here has forgotten Zara. Or what the queen did to her." She hesitated, then added, "Watch Nerezza closely. Her words are poison, and her smile is a blade."

***

The first of the suitors arrived two days later.

Sir Aurell, a handsome but hollow-eyed count from Taryn, was intercepted by Nerezza before Eleanor had the chance to greet him. She laced her voice with flattery and lies, painting Eleanor as a rustic with no grasp of court customs, a girl more suited to stables than statecraft.

By the time Eleanor entered the salon, Aurell's charm had gone brittle. He asked awkward questions about embroidery, land income, and nothing of her past. When she replied plainly, he winced.

The meeting ended with a stiff bow and a promise to "consider other matches."

***

The next guest was Lord Isolde, a revered patron of the arts—unusual, but politically significant. Again, Nerezza struck first, spreading whispers that Eleanor scorned music, had never read a poem, and once mistook a harp for a hunting bow.

Lord Isolde greeted Eleanor with cool skepticism. "Tell me, Lady Labrelle," he said, "what verse stirs your soul?"

Eleanor's mind went blank. Her tongue felt thick. Zara's lullabies swam to the surface, but nothing noble, nothing rehearsed.

"Only silence?" Isolde said, smiling thinly. "A dangerous rhythm for a court full of ears."

\*\*\*

Night after night, Eleanor returned to the quiet corners of the library, shoulders stiff with shame, cheeks flushed with anger. The queen's game was clear: isolate her, diminish her, paint her as a foolish girl clinging to a borrowed crown.

But Eleanor was not a girl anymore.

One evening, while wandering through the eastern wing, she paused beneath a stained-glass window that cast coloured light across the marble floor. It was the same corridor where Zara once worked, where whispers of exile and betrayal first took root.

Her father's footsteps echoed behind her.

He leaned heavily on a cane now. His hands trembled. His colour was poor.

"My daughter," he said quietly. "You are too often alone."

Eleanor turned. "They want me to fail."

"I know," Edgar said. "And I've let them strike in shadows too long."

He reached out and touched her shoulder with a hand that had once held banners in battle. "I see in you a fire they fear. Even your mother, for all her gentleness, had that fire."

"I won't break," Eleanor said. "Not for them."

"Good," Edgar whispered. "Then maybe... I haven't failed you after all."

He smiled, thin and proud.

As he turned away, Eleanor remained still, watching the last rays of sunset catch the silver in his hair.

# CHAPTER 9 - STORM
# AT BRAVETHORNE

N ews of Eleanor's growing prominence—
and Roman's visible affection—reached
the high spires of Bravethorne Castle
within days.

Bravethorne, the ancestral seat of House
Aldren, rose from the fog-laced cliffs of Taryn,
Wonderworth's neighbouring kingdom to the
south. Known for its lush coffee terraces, stone-
carved keeps, and ruthless diplomacy, Taryn was a
land of wealth guarded by sharp minds and sharper
alliances.

In the late evening hush of the solar, warmed by amber lanternlight and the scent of smoked cedar, Prince Roman stood before his father, Duke Aldric of Taryn, heart tangled in longing and loyalty.

"Father," Roman began, voice low but resolute, "I've met a woman unlike any I've known—Lady Eleanor Labrelle of Wonderworth."

Aldric looked up from his parchment. His weathered face bore the gravity of statecraft and bloodlines. "Labrelle," he said, as if weighing the name. "The exiled king's daughter. Edgar's scandal."

"She is more than a name," Roman said, stepping closer. "She is the soul of that kingdom's future. Courage, wisdom—she's endured what others would not survive."

Aldric rose slowly, walking to the tall window that overlooked the moonlit coffee groves. "You are betrothed to Princess Nerezza of Wonderworth," he reminded. "That union was forged to preserve peace and secure the highland trade routes. It binds Taryn to Wonderworth's ports and gives us exclusive control of the mountain-grown coffee exports. If that alliance breaks, so do our revenues —and the balance of power."

Roman's jaw tensed. "So, my heart must yield to

borders and tariffs."

His father turned to face him. "Yes. Because Taryn is not ruled by hearts. It is ruled by strategy. And let's face it, Queen Thanamalice, not Edgar, holds Wonderworth now. If you insult her by shunning her daughter, you invite retaliation. Economic blockade. Diplomatic sabotage. Possibly war."

Roman's hands curled into fists. "So, I must wed a woman I do not love to keep ports open?"

"You must," Aldric said, voice hardening, "if you wish to keep Taryn strong."

He stepped forward, resting a hand on his son's shoulder. "You're no longer just my son. You're Taryn's future. Your heart is yours to grieve. But your duty? That is the crown's."

Roman dropped his gaze. "And if Eleanor takes the throne?"

Aldric paused, then answered honestly. "Then perhaps this all changes. But she has no crown. Only whispers, and enemies cloaked in silks. Until she sits on that throne... *you do not stand beside her.*"

At dawn, Roman walked the terraces behind Bravethorne, the wind cool, the sky mist-silvered.

The coffee trees stretched in precise rows, their garnet cherries ripe for harvest. He moved among the pickers in silence, tasting beans from sun-dried barrels, inspecting parchment for moisture, inhaling the sharp tang of roast and earth.

He remembered the first time Eleanor had tasted Bravethorne coffee—her face wrinkled at the bitterness, then brightened with laughter when she added cream. That memory, simple and bright, hurt more than he expected.

By midday, he was at the coastal warehouse, negotiating shipping contracts with salt-stained merchants, each deal binding Taryn's fortunes more tightly to Wonderworth's unstable crown. He smiled where needed, signed when required, but his thoughts were miles away.

He was walking into a marriage with Nerezza.
And leaving something real behind.

*** 

That evening, in the quiet of his private study, Roman unrolled maps and ledgers—but his gaze drifted to the flame-lit window.

*Eleanor,* he thought. *You are stronger than they know. Perhaps even stronger than I am.*

But strength would not be enough.

Not yet.

# CHAPTER 10 - SCHEMES
# IN SHADOW

By the time word of Prince Roman's quiet return to Bravethorne Castle in Taryn reached Wonderworth, the mood within the palace had soured further. No letters came. No message followed. And Eleanor, though she never spoke of it, felt the hollow ache of distance settle deep in her chest.

She knew Roman had left because of duty. But still —he had left.

The corridors of the castle no longer carried

laughter. They echoed instead with muffled coughs and hurried footsteps. King Edgar had not been seen in public for days, and even the ministers began leaving their chairs empty at council meetings, standing instead in tight clusters outside the royal solar, speaking in whispers Eleanor could feel more than hear.

*"He's fading."*
*"The queen issues orders in his name."*
*"He hasn't signed a decree in a week."*

Even the embroidered tapestries lining the halls seemed muted, their colour dimmed under the flickering torchlight—mourning a king not yet dead.

Eleanor passed them with shoulders square, but she could feel the eyes upon her. Some sympathetic. Some suspicious. All watchful.

\*\*\*

In the queen's solar, the atmosphere was far less subdued.

The air was thick with the scent of lavender and old parchment. Princess Nerezza paced like a caged falcon, her violet-trimmed gown flaring at every frustrated turn.

"He belongs to *me*," she snapped. "And still, he looks

at her. *Still*, he favours her presence."

"Not anymore," Queen Thanamalice replied, calm and venomous. She didn't glance up from the list of appointments before her. "He is gone. Recalled by duty, silenced by obligation. And now, she is alone."

"But they speak of her!" Nerezza hissed. "The nobles, the maids—even the council. Her name rides every corridor. Eleanor. Eleanor. Eleanor!"

Thanamalice finally looked up, her expression flat. "Then we must shift the narrative. Not by protest. But by pressure."

She moved to the window, gazing out at the grey-tinged sky beyond the northern wing. Frost crept along the leaded glass like veins through skin. Below, Eleanor could be seen approaching the infirmary wing—her step steady, her face composed, but her posture bent with invisible weight.

Thanamalice's voice sharpened. "Edgar's days are dwindling. His body weakens. His will is... unmoored. Soon, his hold will fail completely."

She turned back to her daughter. "Until then, we contain her. Not by exile, but by entanglement."

Nerezza raised a brow. "You mean... tire her?"

"I mean bind her. Chain her in golden duties, lace her in velvet expectations. Strip her of freedom under the guise of responsibility. She will have no time to dream, no breath to plan."

The queen unfurled a parchment and read aloud the newly issued order:

"Henceforth, Lady Eleanor Labrelle shall:
— Supervise the king's medicinal rituals each dawn
— Record and register all personal petitions on the king's behalf
— Measure and deliver restorative draughts alongside the healers
— Manage inventory and staff rotations within the royal infirmary
— And by evening, submit compiled reports to the Privy Steward.
Failure to fulfil any task shall result in a summons to the Queen's Chamber."

Nerezza's eyes lit with dark satisfaction. "No time for moonlit dances. No whispered letters. She'll rot in herbs and ink."

***

That morning, Eleanor received the decree with a faint flicker of her brow—but no outward protest.

If this was their latest strategy, then she would meet it head-on.

By dawn, she was kneeling beside her father's sickbed in the infirmary, the scent of valerian root and warmed honey thick in the air. King Edgar smiled faintly when she took his hand, though he no longer had the strength to speak above a whisper.

She measured tonics. Logged prescriptions. Recited the healing blessings Zara had once whispered over her childhood fevers.

The royal physicians, watching from the shadows, nodded in approval. But they did not meet her eyes.

\*\*\*

Elsewhere in the castle, Nerezza orchestrated distractions.

A surprise falcon display in the grand courtyard. A bard from Silverhaven summoned for a poetry recital. A new tapestry unveiled in the eastern hall, glorifying Queen Thanamalice's bloodline. Noble eyes turned away from the infirmary. Ears drifted from Eleanor's name.

But even amid spectacle, someone heard Eleanor's soft laughter from behind the infirmary doors— King Edgar had murmured a jest, and she had answered with warmth.

It echoed further than Nerezza expected.

\*\*\*

That night, Eleanor climbed the stairs to her turret chamber, limbs aching from unrelenting labour, her eyes stinging with fatigue. She closed the door behind her and pressed her forehead to the cool wood.

She did not weep.

Instead, she unclasped the silver pendant at her throat and held it to her lips.

"For Mother. For Father. For the crown."

She collapsed onto the bed, gown unremoved, boots still damp with snowmelt. Sleep claimed her quickly, but unrest stirred in her dreams—Roman's voice, distant. The queen's gaze, cold. Her father's breathing, shallow and fading.

\*\*\*

Far below, in the hush of the solar, Thanamalice stood alone with a glass of wine untouched.

The moonlight cast her reflection across the glass. She smiled—small, precise.

Everything was working. Eleanor was not broken. But she was bending.

And the queen knew... bend far enough, and anything would eventually snap.

# CHAPTER 11
# - FRACTURED
# ALLEGIANCES

Dawn broke over Wonderworth in cold silence.

Eleanor stood alone on the balcony of her turret chamber, the sharp morning air cutting against her cheeks. Below, the courtyard stirred to life: servants rushed between wings, doves scattered from the battlements, and a heavy tension clung to the stones like frost.

She hadn't slept.

The night before had drained her—physically, emotionally, utterly. Her father's breath had wheezed in shallow rasps, and the candlelight beside his bed had burned low. She had left the infirmary only once, just long enough to climb to her chamber, collapse fully clothed across her mattress, and weep into her sleeve.

But now, the world demanded composure.

Then came the sound that twisted her gut.

Hooves. Iron striking stone. The hollow ring of riders entering the palace gates.

She leaned forward, eyes narrowing as she spotted the crest of Taryn—a falcon clutching three black roses—emblazoned on the lead rider's cloak.

Roman.

He dismounted with practiced grace, green eyes shadowed and unreadable. No trumpets, no herald. His return had not been announced to the court. But Eleanor's heart knew before reason did: he hadn't come for ceremony.

He had come for her. Or so she hoped.

Heart hammering, she descended the marble staircase and crossed the frost-kissed courtyard to meet him. He turned at the sound of her steps.

"Your Highness," she greeted, voice steady despite the storm rising inside her.

He bowed stiffly. "Lady Eleanor." His eyes did not meet hers.

Her breath hitched. "You're here... Why?"

"I owed you a word," he said. "A farewell."

"A farewell?" Her voice was barely a whisper. After everything?

"I returned to finalize the coffee accords with the queen," Roman said, voice brittle. "The merchants await my seal. My absence has caused disruption."

"Is that all I am now?" she asked, stepping closer. "Disruption?"

His jaw tightened, and for a moment, something softened in his expression—something wounded and wild. "You know what we shared," he said. "But I cannot let it undo what I am bound to protect."

Eleanor looked away, blinking fast. "So, our night was a moment to you. A single breath in a lifetime of treaties and trade."

"It was more than a moment," he said hoarsely. "But moments end."

Before she could answer, silk whispered behind them.

Princess Nerezza stepped from the archway, her violet gown trailing behind her like spilled ink.

Without hesitation, she looped her arm through Roman's.

"My prince," she purred, "the council awaits us in the solar. Your delay has already stirred questions."

Roman glanced at Eleanor one last time. Regret flickered behind his gaze—but he said nothing. He allowed Nerezza to lead him away, her smile triumphant, her head tipped just enough to glance over her shoulder at Eleanor with gleaming satisfaction.

Eleanor did not move. She watched them disappear down the corridor, their silhouettes framed by the high-arched glass.

Only when the cold truly began to bite did she turn back toward her chambers.

\*\*\*

She locked the door behind her and collapsed against it, her strength finally giving way. Tears broke free, hot and unchecked, tracing silent paths down her cheeks.

She pressed a hand to her chest, feeling the familiar weight of the pendant—the only warmth left.

*He deflowered me,* she thought bitterly. *Brought me to life—and left me like a discarded blossom.*

Her knees gave way, and she sank to the floor, arms wrapped around her legs, fury and sorrow battling for control inside her ribs. She had offered him everything, and now he vanished behind a treaty and a betrothal she'd never had the chance to rival.

*Was it all lies?*
*Was I only ever a pause in his duty?*

No answer came—only the echo of retreating hooves, and the aching void his absence left behind.

But Eleanor would not stay broken.

She rose, slow but sure, and moved to her writing desk. She drew a sheet of parchment, dipped her quill, and wrote:

*Your Highness,*
*The night we shared was a gift I will treasure always.*
*Yet today, I feel your warmth has fled.*
*I wish you success in your duties. May they not demand more than your heart can bear.*
*—Eleanor*

She sealed the note with trembling hands. A farewell unspoken. A bridge unburned.

*** 

In the queen's solar, Thanamalice lowered her spyglass with quiet satisfaction.

From her balcony, she had watched every moment of Roman's arrival—and his departure with Nerezza clinging like ivy.

She sipped her spiced wine slowly, savouring the bitter heat. Everything was falling into place.

"Affections fade," she murmured to no one. "But power remains."

And Eleanor, weakened and alone, had never been easier to isolate.

# CHAPTER 12 - THE MIDNIGHT TRAP

**M**idnight cloaked Wonderworth in frost and silence.

But far across the sea in Bravethorne's shadowed solar, silence shattered with a soft cry.

Roman stood before the hearth, Eleanor's letter clenched in his hand—its words now burned into his memory like a scar.

*The night we shared was a gift I will treasure always. Yet today, I feel your warmth has fled...*

The parchment trembled in his grip. His throat

ached. Guilt gripped his chest with claws.

"I'm a coward," he whispered, voice hoarse. "I left her when she needed me most."

He sank to his knees before the fire, the letter crumpled near his heart. In that moment, the echoes of duty, politics, and alliance crumbled beneath something far more powerful - regret.

Throwing aside his coat, he seized a cloak and hood. He wouldn't wait for daylight.

***

Wind lashed his face as Roman galloped beneath moonlit boughs, tearing through the dense forests of Taryn, his mind a storm of longing and resolve. He crossed the River Wind, its cold spray biting against his legs. By the time the towers of Wonderworth crowned the dark horizon, Roman was soaked in sweat and desperation.

The guards at the eastern gate had long since retired to their posts. Roman slipped past the shadows, hood drawn low, boots silent on cobblestone. He moved like a ghost through servants' halls, past storerooms and kitchens and the familiar scent of ashwood smoke.

At a small alcove near the scullery, he found Mara, the aging housekeeper who had once served Zara Labrelle.

She looked up, startled—but not surprised.

"You came back," she murmured. "She's not slept."

"I must see her," Roman said. "Please."

With a nod, Mara took up her lantern and led him through the hidden stairwell that wound up to the turret chambers.

At the top, she paused outside Eleanor's door. "She's been crying," she said softly. "But she waited."

Roman nodded, brushing his hand over Mara's. "Thank you."

He pushed the door open gently and slipped inside.

\*\*\*

Roman stepped through the half-open door into Eleanor's chamber, the candlelight barely illuminating the edges of the room. The air was heavy with the scent of lavender sweat and fear.

She tossed and turned beneath her covers, her face slick with sweat, her breaths shallow and quick. A low whimper escaped her lips. Her hands clawed the sheets as if trying to hold onto something that wasn't there.

Roman froze at the sight, his expression darkening with concern. He moved closer, slowly, cautiously. Her forehead glistened; her hair tangled against the pillow. She looked like she was being hunted even in her sleep.

He reached out, touched her shoulder.

She jolted upright with a gasp, eyes wide and wild. Her chest heaved as she tried to steady her breath. For a heartbeat, she didn't see him—only the remnants of what chased her in the dark.

"I—" she began, but stopped. The dream clung to her, heavy and vivid.

She had been back in the Outlands. The creature— taller than any tree, its single red eye blazing—had spoken her name again.

She opened her mouth to tell him. To describe the way it had loomed over her, the words it had spoken, how it had promised they would meet again. She had meant to say it. But then her eyes cleared, and she saw who sat in front of her.

Roman.

And just like that, the words slipped away.

Her whole body stilled.

For a long moment, neither of them spoke.

Then her voice broke the silence, low and unsure.

"Roman?"

He knelt beside the bed, eyes pleading. "I had to come. I couldn't leave it like that."

She sat up slowly, the sheet clutched against her chest, her hair tumbling across her shoulders. Her eyes, glassy with sleep and pain, searched his face like she was seeing a ghost. A memory.

"You left," she whispered. "You stood beside her. You walked away while I broke."

"I know," he said softly.

"I gave you everything," she continued, voice cracking. "I had never loved before—not anyone. And you were the first man to look at me like I was worth something more than a secret. And then you left."

Tears welled in her eyes.

"You broke something in me, Roman. I need to know why."

He looked down, ashamed. "I was afraid."

"Of what?" she asked.

He raised his eyes. "Of losing everything I was raised to protect. My kingdom. My family's trade. My father's respect. Nerezza's alliance. I thought if I stayed with you, I would unravel everything my name was built on."

"And so, you sacrificed me instead?" she asked, the tremble in her voice sharper now. "You let me believe I was just a moment. A distraction."

"No," he said fiercely. "You were never a distraction.

You are the only thing that has ever felt real to me."

She said nothing. Her breath hitched.

"I've done things by duty my entire life," he continued. "I know how to follow orders, how to keep peace, how to wear a crown that doesn't fit. But with you... I was just Roman. Not a prince. Not a pawn. And it terrified me, because I wanted it more than I've ever wanted anything."

Silence fell again.

Then, Eleanor slowly released the sheet clutched at her chest and wiped at her eyes.

"I needed to hear that," she whispered. "Because I was starting to believe I was foolish. That loving you was a mistake."

He reached for her hand. "It wasn't. I promise you."

Her fingers hovered in the air for a moment—then curled around his.

"I forgive you," she said, voice thick. "But don't ever make me question myself like that again. I am not a mistake."

"You're not," he said. "You're the one thing I've done right."

She let out a long breath, trembling slightly as he reached to hold her.

"I missed you," she whispered. "I hated that I missed you."

"I missed you with every breath," he murmured, brushing his forehead to hers.

Their kiss came gently at first—an answer, not a question. And then, with slow urgency, the need between them deepened. This time, not in heat or desperation, but in deliberate devotion.

They made love with reverence—hands searching, hearts open, the pain of the past soothed in every whispered promise. Eleanor's body welcomed him not as a stranger, but as the man who had returned —who had chosen her again.

And afterward, in the hush of dawn, Eleanor rested her head against his chest, their legs tangled beneath the sheets.

Roman stroked her hair and whispered, "I'll never leave again."

She nodded against his skin. "Good. Because if you do... I won't wait for you next time." *Would she?*

He smiled faintly, pressing a kiss to her temple. "Fair."

*** 

But below, in the hedges near her turret, a pair of

eyes watched.

Nerezza stood cloaked in shadow, her breath caught in her throat as she saw their silhouettes melt into one.

Her jaw tightened. Her fingers curled around the hilt of her ceremonial dagger.

*Her hear ached. She fought the tears welling up in her eyes. She has him now.*

But she wouldn't for long.

Nerezza turned and vanished into the darkness, rage coiled in her chest.

If Eleanor Labrelle had stolen her crown, she would wear it over ashes.

# CHAPTER 13 -
# BETRAYALS AT DUSK

I n the hushed days that followed their secret reunion, Eleanor and Roman clung to each other like two souls defying the tide.

Their stolen moments were fragile things—shared whispers beneath rose-draped archways, lingering touches between tall library shelves. In the warmth of the reading room or during candlelit chess games that neither tried to win, their love deepened—quiet, unspoken, but undeniable.

Roman reaffirmed his vow with steady hands and unwavering eyes. "I will annul the betrothal," he said. "At the next council session, I'll announce it myself. Nerezza's claim will end. I'll choose you—publicly, without shame."

Eleanor's breath caught, her fingers trembling as they traced his promise. "And then?"

He smiled, brushing a lock of hair from her brow. "Then we plan the life we were meant to live. A family. Peace. A future not built on secrecy, but on truth."

For the first time in weeks, hope bloomed in Eleanor's chest. But it was delicate. Brittle.

Every laugh between them was softened by the shadow of discovery. Every touch, haunted by the awareness of Nerezza's cold, burning stare through the palace walls.

Still, they believed they could survive it.

Until the whispers began.

***

Servants in the halls paused mid-task to exchange knowing glances. In the kitchens, spoons slipped from hands, and pans clanged louder than usual. Grooms in the stables murmured of unusual tension in the air—horses neighed and shifted nervously, as if catching scent of some unspoken upheaval.

Jasper the Herald had been summoned.

He was seen sharpening his quill, preparing parchment. The kingdom's master of announcements never rose before dawn unless a declaration of great weight was to be made.

Roman had requested the proclamation be prepared: a formal renunciation of his betrothal to Nerezza, and a statement of intent to wed Lady Eleanor Labrelle.

In a quiet gallery just above the eastern terrace, Eleanor clutched Roman's hand. "What have they heard already?" she whispered.

Roman's jaw was tense, his voice low. "Everything, most likely. But I no longer care. Let them speak— I'll give them something worth saying."

Eleanor's smile was sad. "Then speak it quickly."

***

That evening, beneath the pale light of the moon, Nerezza found Roman alone in the stone garden near the southern wing. He held the scroll in his hand—the formal declaration. His shoulders were squared. His mind was made.

She approached slowly, her expression fragile, her silk gown brushing the gravel like falling petals.

"I've heard," she said softly. "You mean to announce

it tomorrow."

"I do," Roman said, not unkindly. "The lie ends now."

There was pain in her eyes. "Please," she said, stepping closer, her voice trembling with practiced ache. "One day. That's all I ask."

He turned toward her, uncertain.

"Let me speak first," she continued. "Let me be the one to step aside—to show the court that I release you, not the other way around. Spare us both the scandal of rejection."

Her fingers brushed his arm, lingering—a touch both pleading and possessive.

"Alright, just one day," she said again.

Roman hesitated. Eleanor's face flickered in his mind. So did Aldric's warnings. And Nerezza's years of dutiful silence.

"One day," he repeated.

Nerezza smiled faintly, then stepped away. "Thank you."

***

That night, as the castle slept, Nerezza set her plan in motion.

Two letters, each written in a different hand.

One, forged in Eleanor's elegant script, summoned Roman to the lighthouse at the eastern quay, under the guise of a secret meeting with loyal nobles willing to support his proclamation.

The other, penned with delicate emotion, appeared in Eleanor's chamber—a message claiming to be from Roman himself, asking her to meet him at the harbour at dawn, for one last moment before they told the world.

Mara never saw who delivered the letter. Only that it was left beneath the door.

Eleanor read it by candlelight, her heart leaping.

It was brief. Tender. Familiar.

*Come to the port at first light. Just us. Before the storm begins, let me remind you why we weather it.*
*—R.*

Exhausted but moved, she placed the letter gently beside her pillow and drifted into a restless sleep, imagining him waiting for her by the sea, the sun rising behind him.

*** 

High above the courtyard, Nerezza watched from the second-story window, the candlelight casting shadows across her sharp features.

She pressed a palm to her chest, her breath shallow, her lips trembling.

*Soon, she will vanish. He will grieve. And he will find me waiting.*

Her tears were real. But so was her resolve.

In the silence of her chamber, with the ink still drying on Eleanor's forged letter, Nerezza's heart split in two.

And only one half was still capable of love.

# CHAPTER 14 -
# COURT OF ASHES

R oman rose before the sixth bell, heart thrumming with anticipation. Dawnlight spilled through the coloured panes of his chamber, casting emerald and gold across the polished stone floor.

On his table lay the note from Eleanor, its words etched into his memory:

*Meet me at the Eastcliff Sanctuary at first light. Just us. I want to see the sun rise with you—before the court takes us back.*
*—E.*

A private place. Sacred. Old. It suited her.

Roman dressed with care—not for ceremony, but for her. White linen, a forest-green jerkin, tall leather boots, and his cloak pinned by Bravethorne's crest. Under the white linen, the cut of his jerkin pressed against broad pectorals and tapered to a narrow waist, the lines of his muscles visible even beneath fabric—each movement controlled, each breath measured by the strength that had carried him across five kingdoms. At his belt, he carried the rolled parchment of the proclamation—the one that would end his betrothal and declare his intent to wed Eleanor.

*Let her hear it from my lips first,* he thought.

He mounted Bayspur, his grey stallion, and rode swiftly through the waking countryside. Mist clung to the trees, and the hills glowed gold as the sun crested the horizon.

*She'll be waiting,* he told himself. *She always believed in me.*

\*\*\*

Elsewhere, within the palace's quiet north wing, Eleanor stood at her window, clutching the letter she'd received under her door.

*Come to the eastern port at first light. No one will follow. I want you to see me in the place where it all*

*began—where I knew it was you.*
*—R.*

The harbour. The sea. It made sense in its own way —Roman was from Taryn, born to trade winds and salt spray. It was the kind of farewell to secrecy he would choose. She pressed the page to her lips.

He was ready.

She slipped into a gown of soft rose silk, woven with faint embroidery like waves curling along the hem. She pinned her hair back with fresh palace roses and fastened her cloak without trembling. Her chest swelled with nervous joy.

He loved her. And today, he would prove it.

\*\*\*

Roman reached the Eastcliff Sanctuary just as the sun broke above the horizon. Sea winds rushed through the crumbling stone arches and ivy-veiled alcoves, carrying salt and birdsong.

He dismounted, cloak billowing behind him. He searched every shadow. Every tree.

But she wasn't there.

His eyes scanned the grove. No footprints. No silhouette. No Eleanor.

He waited.

Minutes passed.

Then an hour.

His chest tightened.

He reread the note again. Had he misunderstood? Was he too early? Too late?

His hope withered as the wind pulled at the hem of his cloak. He stood in the empty sanctuary, alone.

*\*\**

Down at the eastern port, Eleanor stepped onto the mist-slick pier.

The sun glittered on the waves, and boats creaked softly in their moorings. Fishermen hauled nets, and the scent of brine hung in the air.

But there was no Roman.

She walked to the farthest dock, eyes darting between each passing figure. Sailors. Traders. No green cloak. No dark hair.

She waited.

Then paced.

Then waited again.

Her heart twisted.

*\*\*\**

Back at the palace, whispers stirred like wind through dry leaves.

"Lady Eleanor left before dawn."
"The prince was seen riding east."
"They say he was carrying a scroll…"

At the high table, Queen Thanamalice sipped her spiced wine, face a mask of serenity.

"They will return," she said lightly. "They always do."

But in her heart, she knew - they would not return the same.

*\*\*\**

The sun had crowned the sky. The sanctuary stood silent—overgrown stone archways, ivy-swept walls, and a single marble bench bathed in light.

She *still* wasn't there.

He had paced the clearing, circled the grove, searched behind every pillar.

Nothing.

A knot formed in his chest.

He pulled the note from his pouch, scanning the lines again. They were her words. Her handwriting. Her tenderness.

But now, they read like a goodbye.

He waited hours and hours.

And when the sun sat high above him and his voice had gone hoarse from silence, Roman mounted his horse and rode back—slowly, empty-handed.

***

At the harbour, Eleanor stood alone on the weathered planks, her dawn-rose gown dulled by salt spray and time.

Hours had passed since sunrise.

The sun now hung high in the sky, casting harsh white light across the harbour. Its warmth barely touched her skin. The carriage that had brought her here had long since vanished, swallowed by the maze of streets behind the warehouses.

She was still waiting. Still hoping.

*He must be searching for me,* she thought again,

though the conviction had long bled from her voice. She'd waited too long to still believe in certainty—but her heart clung stubbornly to what remained.

Each time hoofbeats echoed along the stone quay, she turned—hope flaring, her breath catching—only to see strangers. Traders. Sailors. Men carrying crates, women rolling barrels.

No Roman.

No emerald cloak. No flash of Bravethorne silver.

Just the whisper of the sea and the sting of betrayal wrapping around her like a second skin.

She leaned against a crate, the scent of fish and brine turning her stomach. Her fingers clenched the note she had believed was his, the ink beginning to smudge where salt met sorrow.

Tears blurred her vision.

*He said he loved me.*

*He said he would never leave again.*

Her throat tightened as panic crept in. Her knees wobbled beneath her, and she pressed a trembling hand to her collarbone to steady her breath.

*What have I done? What did I believe in?*

A low whistle interrupted her spiralling thoughts.

From behind a leaning mast, two familiar figures approached: Halvric and Norn, the traveling jesters once known for juggling apples in the palace courtyard, now dressed in sea-worn cloaks.

Halvric spoke softly, voice too kind. "My lady, forgive the intrusion. You shouldn't linger here. The quay's no place for royalty alone."

Norn nodded, eyes cast downward. "There've been whispers—bandits along the shoreline. We're here to take you somewhere safe. The queen's orders."

Eleanor hesitated, heart thudding. She thinks she knew them. Even laughed at their antics in the great hall.

And she was alone. Roman hadn't come. The docks were empty of all promises.

Her voice barely rose above a whisper. "You've seen him? Prince Roman?"

The men exchanged a glance that flickered with guilt. Halvric offered a half-bow. "Only the queen's request, milady. She feared something like this."

Something broke in Eleanor. She nodded, slowly.

They offered their arms. And though her soul screamed against it, her body complied.

***

They led her through a winding alley between warehouse walls, the air thick with tar and seaweed. The dock bustle faded behind them, replaced by quiet—too quiet.

Inside a dim warehouse near the water's edge, Halvric gestured toward a crate to rest.

"We'll sort out *what we need to sort out.* Just around the bend," he said gently. "You'll be safe, milady. Please wait here."

Eleanor sank onto the edge of a crate, cradling her hands in her lap. Her eyes burned. Her chest felt hollow.

She did not see Norn slip out the back.

***

Moments later, Norn returned, his voice breathless.

"The tide's too low for the boat. But we've arranged a ship—it sails now. Just beyond the wharf. We must hurry."

Eleanor blinked, confused. "A ship?"

"A merchant vessel. It will take you inland. The queen insisted," he added quickly.

Uncertain but too drained to argue, Eleanor followed.

They led her down a narrow dock toward a waiting vessel, its sails already bloated with wind. The crew shouted, ropes flung, barrels rolled into place.

It was too fast. Too coordinated.

Eleanor's steps slowed. "Wait... this isn't—this isn't right—"

She turned to leave.

But Halvric and Norn stepped behind her.

Blocking her path.

Their smiles were gone.

Eleanor's breath hitched. "This isn't what I agreed to."

Norn's voice cracked. "Forgive us."

Halvric wouldn't meet her eyes. "We have our orders."

Orders? Orders from who? What is going on? Thought Eleanor. The queen? Roman?!

Then hands—strong, unfamiliar—grabbed her arms. She screamed, the sound muffled by the crash of waves and cries of gulls. She fought, twisted, bit —but they were prepared.

The gangplank lifted behind her.

The ship groaned. The wind shifted.

And the quay slipped away.

\*\*\*

From the deck, Eleanor watched the towers of Wonderworth blur into mist.

"No... no, please!" she cried, straining against her captors.

But the shore receded, and no one called back.

Only the steady rhythm of the oars. Only the wind's cruel silence.


Tears streaked her cheeks as the only home she'd ever known disappeared behind her—and with it, the man she had loved, who would now believe she had abandoned him. Or did he abandon her?

Eleanor sank to her knees on the deck, breath wracked by sobs, her fingers clawing the salt-stained wood.

Her heart shattered anew—not from absence, but from silence.


And across the sea, the future loomed—unseen, unknown, and without mercy.

# CHAPTER 15 -
# BROKEN VOWS

R oman's hope had burned bright at first light —clear, strong, and absolute.

But by midmorning, that hope had collapsed into a hollow ache.

He had waited beneath the pale-rose arch in the Eastcliff Sanctuary until the sun rose high and hot, until his voice was hoarse from calling her name into the empty garden. Eleanor never came.

His thoughts spun. *Was she delayed? Had something happened? Or... had she simply changed her mind?*

By the time he reached Wonderworth's gates again, dread had taken full root in his chest. He dismounted before the guards could open the gate fully, rushing inside with urgency pounding through his blood.

"Where is she?" he demanded. "Princess Eleanor Labrelle—has she returned?"

The guards exchanged troubled glances. One hesitated, then said, "Your Highness... there are whispers."

Roman's stomach dropped. "What whispers?"

A steward nearby stepped forward, uneasily wringing a scroll in his hands. "We have only gossip, my lord, but... someone claims Lady Eleanor was seen at dawn boarding a private carriage. It was heading east."

"East?" Roman's voice broke. "Where? To Taryn? Taryn?"

"We cannot confirm, sire," the steward replied gently. "But some say she fled."

Roman staggered back a step, winded by the blow. *Fled?*
The word echoed like a knife in his ribs.

Had she changed her mind after all? Had their

night meant nothing?

He turned without another word and stormed through the palace halls, boots slamming against marble tile. Courtiers fell silent in his wake. The throne room loomed—dim, cool, and cavernous.

Jasper the Herald approached with a scroll in hand, his voice unsteady. "Your Highness. There is... official word. A letter from the Council's clerk. It claims Lady Eleanor has withdrawn her petition to the throne."

Roman froze.

The breath in his lungs died.

"What?" he whispered.

"She has renounced her claim, my lord," Jasper said, avoiding his eyes. "And..." He swallowed hard. "It is said she has left Wonderworth entirely. Possibly to marry abroad."

Roman stood motionless for a long moment.

Then the scroll dropped from his hand.

He sank to his knees at the foot of the dais, hands trembling as he pressed them to his face. *No. Not again. Not like this.*

She had forgiven him. She had said she loved him. She had asked him to meet her—and then never came.

Had he been too late?

Or had she been lying?

The walls of the great hall blurred, and the whispers grew louder around him. Betrayal. Flight. Shame.

Somewhere deep inside, something cracked.

\*\*\*

He left the hall wordless, shoulders hunched and eyes hollow.

Outside, Bayspur neighed as Roman stumbled into the courtyard. He caught the reins and leaned against the stallion's shoulder, drawing breath like a drowning man gasping for air.

But he didn't ride.

Not this time.

\*\*\*

From a silk-draped balcony above, Nerezza watched in silence.

His despair hung over the stones like a ghost.

She descended the stairs quietly and crossed the

courtyard. Her eyes were calm, her pace graceful, her voice soft when she spoke:

"Roman... my prince."

He didn't look at her.

"She's gone," he rasped. "She lied. After everything... she left."

Nerezza stepped closer and gently placed a hand on his chest. "I'm so sorry," she whispered. "Come inside. Let me sit with you awhile."

Roman let himself be led, too numb to protest. Through a hidden corridor and into the queen's solar, where candlelight softened the world and silenced the echoes of loss.

\*\*\*

Nerezza poured him a goblet of deep red wine, fragrant with cinnamon and honey.

"Drink," she said softly. "It will ease your heart."

Roman obeyed. The wine went down warm and sharp. A second glass followed, then a third. He said nothing as the haze of drink dulled the sharpest edge of grief.

When at last his hand trembled too much to lift the goblet, Nerezza caught it.

"Come," she murmured. "Rest now."

She led him through another door, up a narrow stair to her private rooms—candles flickering, velvet sheets turned down, the perfume of lavender and myrrh thick in the air.

There, she guided him out of his cloak and boots, then eased him onto the bed, where he sank into down-stuffed pillows like a man falling through sleep.

Roman's eyes drifted shut. His breathing slowed.

Nerezza knelt beside him and brushed a lock of hair from his brow.

"I'll take care of you now," she whispered. "No more betrayal. No more pain."

She kissed his temple, and though her smile wavered, her resolve did not.

As Roman slipped into a dreamless stupor, Nerezza stood.

Her hand tightened around the empty goblet.

And in the silence, the seeds of a false future were sown.

# CHAPTER 16 - SALT
# BETWEEN STARS

T he sea stretched into eternity.

Eleanor stood at the bow, her fingers clenched around the rigging as the ship cut across grey-green waves. Days blurred into one another. Then weeks. Then longer still. Time became nothing more than the tilt of the horizon and the wind in her hair.

She had stopped asking questions.

At first, she had shouted and screamed and begged to be returned. But no one listened—or if they did, they pretended not to understand. Even Halvric and Norn, who now lingered guiltily near her, had gone quiet. Their jokes became few. Their laughter faded.

The only constant was the sea.

Each night, as the stars wheeled overhead, Eleanor tried to make sense of what had happened. *Had Roman abandoned her? Had she misunderstood? Had she been foolish to believe she was loved?*

The memory of his touch made her breath catch. His whispered promises tangled with the salt in her throat. *You said you'd never leave me.*

But she couldn't cry anymore. The grief had gone too deep. Now, it lived in her bones.

She no longer knew whether she'd been betrayed… or simply lost.

And she was too tired to find the answer.

***

When they finally reached land, Eleanor was pale and thin, her hair windswept, her voice soft as linen folding.

The ship docked beneath towering cliffs, where Kaerleon's spires glinted like silver spears against a sky swept clean by storms. She did not know the name of the kingdom—only that the air smelled of lemons and firewood, and the stone streets were smooth underfoot.

No one announced her arrival.

No fanfare. No suspicion. She was simply... there.

A stranger in a foreign land.

She was given no titles. No chambers of her own. Only a borrowed shift, a tray of tea, and instructions to assist in the palace's laundry wing.

\*\*\*

King Halric first saw her in the orchard garden.

She was kneeling near the fountain, her hands submerged in cool water as she rinsed linens. The late afternoon light touched her hair with gold. Her back was straight despite the weight of labour. There was a calmness to her that caught his attention immediately—not weakness, but a kind of noble sadness.

He asked the steward at his side, "Who is she?"

"A new girl from the docks, Sire," the steward said. "No name. She was brought aboard a merchant ship last week with two Kaerleon-born deckhands. She's quiet. Obedient."

Halric tilted his head, watching as she wrung the cloth with elegant precision. "She doesn't move like a servant."

"No, Sire. But she asks for nothing."

"See that she serves in the west wing. In my household."

"Sire?"

"I would speak with her. In time."

That evening, Eleanor was summoned to the west wing of the palace. She expected reprimand. Instead, she was guided into a small library bathed in lamplight.

There, King Halric stood beside a carved desk, rolling a plum between his fingers. He was tall and broad-shouldered, with silvery-dark hair swept back from a high forehead and thoughtful steel-grey eyes that softened around the corners when he smiled

"You're not Kaerleon-born," he said, not unkindly.

She curtseyed. "No, Your Majesty."

"And yet you speak our tongue well."

"I was taught many tongues growing up," she answered softly.

Halric's eyes narrowed with interest. "Where did you learn to stand like that?"

She faltered. "I... don't know."

He smiled gently. "That is not an ordinary answer."

Eleanor lowered her gaze. "I'm not certain I am ordinary, Sire."

There was a long pause.

Then Halric gestured to the seat across from him. "Would you sit with me a while?"

*** 

From that day forward, he invited her often—not as a maid, not as a ward, but as a companion.


They walked the gardens in the cool mornings, his hands behind his back, hers clasped at her waist. Beneath the linen of his tunic, she could just discern the steady line of his collarbone and the lean strength of his arms—an understated power that belied the velvet generosity of his voice. He spoke of Kaerleon's great migration, of how the kingdom had once been flooded and rebuilt stone by stone.

"You speak little," he remarked one day, as they passed a trellis heavy with jasmine.

"I've said enough to people who didn't listen," she replied.

Halric glanced at her, then nodded once. "Then I will listen. When you are ready."

\*\*\*

Some evenings, they read together—books from her past, rediscovered in Kaerleon's vast library. When she reached for a volume of folktales from Thaloria, her hand trembled.

"You miss it," Halric said.

"Sometimes I wonder if it ever existed at all," she answered, her voice hollow.

He did not press her.

\*\*\*

Over time, Eleanor found herself watching him more closely. He was fair, but not performative. Warm, but never forward. He carried the burden of rulership with quiet grace—and for the first time, she saw power without cruelty.

One rainy afternoon, they sat in the map room. A fire crackled between them.

Halric turned a crystal sphere between his palms and said, "You still don't trust me."

"I don't know how to trust anyone anymore," she whispered.

He set the sphere down. "Then let us not begin with trust. Let us begin with kindness."

\*\*\*

Still, Eleanor kept secrets.

She did not tell him that she was taken against her will.

She did not speak of Roman.

She did not speak of the betrayal. Or the crown. Or the truth that once, she might have ruled.


But in the quiet moments, in the way she stood beside him or accepted his silence, she allowed herself to feel something she hadn't in months:

Safe.

# CHAPTER 17 -
# REDEMPTION AND
# RECKONING

**W**onderworth was unravelling.

The markets in Goldsquare had withered to a hushed murmur. The silk stalls, once teeming with outlanders and silver-tongued merchants, stood half-empty. The coffee district, once the lifeblood of Wonderworth's trade routes, lay in ruin—its fields scorched, warehouses abandoned, sacks of unroasted beans left to rot in rain-leaking sheds.

The beasts had returned.

Not in rumour. Not in prophecy. In flesh and fury.

They had crossed the Waterlock border in packs, shadowing the broken treaty like carrion birds drawn to blood. No one knew exactly when the breach began—perhaps weeks after Eleanor vanished, perhaps before—but it had gone unnoticed in the chaos that followed the King's decline. Lawlessness and desperation opened the gates. Farmers, priced out of their own markets by Queen Thanamalice's brutal tariffs, began slipping across the forbidden border to trade in secret, hoping to find fairer deals in the east.

But the Outlands do not forgive trespass.

The beasts—massive, mottled things with hides like burnt iron and eyes that shimmered like molten pitch—descended first on the border posts. Then on the trade caravans. Then on the fields.

They did not kill to eat.

They destroyed to send a message.

Coffee was the first to fall. Whole plantations flattened overnight, fields trampled, and rootstock torn from the soil. Crops that had taken decades to cultivate vanished in a single raid. Harvesters fled inland. Traders vanished mid-route. What little coffee remained was hoarded or hidden, and those who tried to smuggle beans across the borders were often found days later, bodies twisted and drained of blood, strange claw marks carved deep into the bark of nearby trees.

Whispers said the beasts moved with unnatural speed—one moment smoke on the horizon, the next a blur of claws and teeth in the dark. Entire villages went silent overnight. Stone walls did nothing. Steel barely slowed them.

And worst of all: they were multiplying.

Every kingdom east of the Orwain River now tightened its borders. Silverhaven refused refugees. Thaloria demanded tribute for safe passage. Even Taryn, once a close ally, had begun building walls along the shared ridge.

Wonderworth stood alone.

The Queen's coffers had run dry trying to replace the failed harvests. Her ministers bickered over phantom trade routes. No envoys had returned from the Outlands. And still, the beasts came.

In the lower courts, rebellion stirred. Farmers gathered in secret, their eyes hollow, their pockets empty. Artisans stopped producing. Ships rotted in the harbors, waiting for goods that would never arrive. Every merchant's tongue now carried the same bitter truth: the kingdom's greatest export was gone, and with it, its future.

Meanwhile, the Queen refused to loosen her grip.

Prices soared. Currencies were devalued. The black market thrived while children starved in the shadow of the palace. And all the while, Queen Thanamalice dined on imported fruit, refusing to acknowledge the plague moving steadily westward.

Some said it was a punishment—from gods long silenced. Others said it was something worse.

A reckoning.

\*\*\*

Eleanor's days in Kaerleon bloomed like a flower slowly coaxed from frost.

Dawn found her walking among citrus groves, sunlight breaking through the mist, her bare fingers grazing the smooth skin of ripening fruit.

King Halric often joined her—never commanding, always near. He asked questions about grafting and weather, about grain fermentation and how her mother brewed medicine from pine bark. He never asked where she was from, never once pushed for truths she wasn't ready to share. And for that, Eleanor was grateful.

In Halric's presence, she rediscovered something that had been stripped away back in Wonderworth: dignity. He gave her roles that mattered—first in the storerooms, then advising on seasonal crop distribution, and finally, to her surprise, hosting visiting envoys in the candlelit great hall beneath murals of Kaerleon's peaceful founding.

There was no crown on her head, yet somehow, she had power again. Not the kind granted by title but earned through quiet consistency.

In the evenings, they walked together beneath colonnades lit by fireflies and lanterns. He told her stories of old rulers who listened instead of warring. She told him of stars named by sailors, and how her mother used to mix salt with lavender to ease fevers.

One night, beneath the arching sky, Halric paused and turned to her.

"You feel like someone I was always meant to meet," he said softly. "Even if I don't yet know who you truly are."

Eleanor's breath caught.

She looked away. "I don't know who I am either... not anymore."

He didn't press her. Just took her hand and let the

silence speak instead.

***

The breeze had changed.

Eleanor stood on the outer balcony of Kaerleon's citadel, a shawl wrapped around her shoulders, staring out across the vineyards that rolled into morning mist. The sky was peach gold. The air smelled of stone, thyme, and something else.

Smoke.

A servant had whispered of fires two days east. Another had mentioned trade ships rerouted to avoid "monster-haunted" ports. And just yesterday, she had passed a merchant in the courtyard arguing over the price of dried beans—*coffee*, she realized, once the coin hit the ground and the name slipped in a hissed curse.

Coffee. The lifeblood of Wonderworth's trade.

Now scarce. Vanishing. Burning.

"Beasts," someone had muttered behind closed doors. "From the Outlands. The old laws are broken."

When Eleanor heard the whispers—when the first servant murmured the word "beasts"—her blood ran cold.

She was in the east corridor of Kaerleon's upper wing when she overheard two guards talking about a village near the Waterlock border that had vanished overnight. No survivors. Just shattered stones and claw marks in the earth. They said it was the same as before. The same as the Outlands.

She recalled all her sleepless nights.

The moment she closed her eyes, it returned: the clearing shrouded in mist, the cold breath of the creature on her skin, its voice speaking her name.

*"Daughter of Zara. I will remember your scent."*

She would always wake up with a start, drenched in sweat, heart racing. Her screams would die in her throat, but her mind remained trapped in that memory. This time, however, Eleanor truly felt afraid.

Not just of what was coming. But of what remembered her.

And now they had come again.

She gripped the stone railing. Part of her wanted to turn away, pretend Kaerleon's peace could hold. But peace was a luxury built on other people's suffering.

She knew that now.

If the treaty had been broken, if the Outlands had risen… it meant Wonderworth was falling. It meant her father the King might be in danger. It meant Roman might be in danger.

Or already lost.

She shivered a bit at the thought that she was still so concerned about his welfare. After all this time.

Her chest ached with a familiar mixture of guilt and yearning.

She'd accepted her fate and remained in Kaerleon to survive and to live without heartbreak and pain and the stress that came with it. But survival wasn't the same as justice. Or healing. Or home.

And Kaerleon, kind as it was, had never really been hers.

She glanced down at the orchard path, where King Halric was speaking to a visiting envoy from Isendra. They bowed to her as they passed, but she didn't return it. Her thoughts were too far away —across the sea, across the ruins of a crumbling crown.

*If the beasts are loose, no one is safe.*
Not her. Not Roman.
Not anyone.

\*\*\*

But across the sea, the silence was heavy with loss.

Wonderworth had become brittle. Without its heir, the crown sat heavy on poisoned roots. Queen Thanamalice's greed tore through the six kingdoms, strangling trade and friendships with crushing tariffs. Port warehouses swelled with goods no one could afford. Roads fell quiet. Letters stopped arriving.

And Prince Roman, once the kingdom's heartbeat, drifted like a leaf on a dying tree.

Grief had hollowed him. Court rumours gnawed at his name. Some said Eleanor had fled with Sir Benedict. Others whispered that she had never loved him at all.

He believed none of them. But he no longer had the strength to argue.

The only thing he believed in was the memory of her voice in the moonlight. *"I've waited so long for this."*

When news came that King Edgar had died—alone, calling for the daughter he never saw again—Roman locked himself in the old king's solar and screamed into the silence. The grief was unbearable. But worse still was the shame.

*I was meant to protect her.*
I failed them both.

Nerezza found him there, slouched at his father's writing desk, knuckles white around an untouched goblet.

"You're pathetic," she hissed, her voice like broken glass. "Once, you were a prince. Now you're a ghost."

Roman didn't look at her.

She moved closer, skirts brushing the stone. "Do you want her back?"

That caught him.

His eyes rose, sharp. "What are you talking about?"

"I know where she is," Nerezza said, sweet and slow. "I've always known. But you lost the right to ask the moment you chose her over your duty."

In a flash, Roman stood. Before she could react, he was across the room. His hand clamped around her throat, lifting her just enough that her heels barely kissed the floor.

Her breath hitched. She clawed at his wrist.

His voice was ice. "Tell me where she is, Nerezza. Or I swear, I will end you before the guards can reach the door."

Her eyes flared in panic, her composure cracking.

"You wouldn't—"

"Don't test me," he growled. "Not with her."

Seconds passed. She choked on silence.

Then she nodded, the smallest, most furious motion.

Roman let go. She crumpled to the floor, coughing, glaring up at him with hatred.

"You've become a monster," she spat.

"No," he said. "I've become a man with nothing left to lose."

She wiped her mouth with the back of her hand, then forced a brittle smile. "Fine. I'll tell you. But I want something in return."

He narrowed his eyes. "What?"

"You'll give me what I asked for before," she said. "An heir. You get me pregnant, and I'll tell you where she is."

Roman's jaw clenched. "You're disgusting."

"You want her or not?" Nerezza hissed. "This is the price."

A long, searing pause.

Finally, his shoulders dropped, and his voice came low, guttural. "Fine. You'll have what you want. But if you lie to me—if she's harmed—there won't be a corner of this realm safe for you."

She smiled, cold and victorious. "Deal."

\*\*\*

That night, the queen's wing of Wonderworth

glowed with a low amber light. The door to Princess Nerezza's chamber opened without a knock.

Roman entered, still clad in the same cloak he'd worn at council, dust from the stables clinging to his boots. He didn't speak. Didn't look around. He just stood there, still and unreadable.

Nerezza waited, emerged in wine-red silk that clung to her slender waist and flared at her hips, pale skin almost luminescent beneath the flicker of torchlight. Her jet-black hair was braided down her back, framing high cheekbones and a pair of emerald eyes that glinted with both command and cold calculation. She rose from the chaise as if in a trance.

"You came," she said.

Roman gave a slow nod. "I said I would."

"And you meant it?"

His eyes met hers. "I want to know where she is."

A beat.

Then Nerezza approached, taking his cloak from his shoulders and letting it fall to the floor. She undid the fastenings of his jerkin with slow fingers. Roman didn't stop her.

But he didn't help either.

She guided him to the edge of the bed. "Lie down,"

she whispered.

He obeyed—woodenly. Nerezza climbed atop him, straddling his hips, her palms pressed to his chest.

Still, he didn't touch her.

Nerezza leaned close, lips hovering just above his. "Think only of me," she said, almost pleading.

But Roman's gaze was distant, glazed. His breath shallow. His hands, though resting at her waist, didn't grip. Didn't move.

She kissed him. Soft at first. Then deeper. Desperate. She pulled at his belt, then froze.

His body did not respond.

Not in the way she needed.

Nerezza pulled back, chest heaving. "Roman?"


Silence.

Her voice cracked. "You promised. You said you'd give me what I asked."

"I'm trying," he said, barely above a whisper. "I am."

"You're not here," she hissed, standing abruptly. "You're somewhere else. With *her*."

Roman sat up, eyes tortured. "I want to know where she is, Nerezza. I need to know. But I can't—" He ran a hand through his hair, jaw clenching. "My mind is full of her. Even when I try... it's her I see. Not you."

Nerezza's eyes shimmered with rage—and something more vulnerable.

"You're a liar," she spat. "You lied to me."

"I didn't lie," he said hoarsely. "I came here. I said I'd try. I *tried*."

She shoved him hard in the chest. "But you couldn't go through with it, could you? Because you don't want me. Because no matter what I offer, I'm never enough."

Roman looked up at her, face pale with guilt. "This isn't about enough. It's about truth."

"You want the truth?" she screamed. "She's gone. And you'll never find her. Not unless I *tell you*. And I won't. Not now."

Roman stood, reaching for her arm. "Please. Don't do this."

Tears spilled down Nerezza's cheeks. "I loved you," she whispered. "I waited. I tried to be everything. And still, you close your eyes and see her."

Roman didn't deny it.

"I'm sorry," he said softly. "But you're asking me to betray myself just to earn a sliver of what you're holding hostage."

"I'm asking for a child!" she shouted, fists clenched. "A kingdom! A future! You act like that's a crime."

She sobbed once, turning her back to him.

His voice broke as he said, "If you ever truly loved me… then tell me where she is."

Nerezza turned to him with fire in her eyes.

"I *do* love you. That's why I *won't* tell you. Because even now, with me in your arms, you're still chasing her ghost. Let it haunt you."

She threw his cloak at him.

"Get out."

***

The sun had not yet risen when Roman left the palace.

But it wasn't just Eleanor that pulled him east.

It was the unravelling of Wonderworth itself.

He had watched it rot from the inside—watched the Queen cling to her velvet throne while smoke rose from the trade routes. Watched ministers argue over tariffs as if numbers could ward off claws. Watched entire towns empty out overnight after the beasts came, monstrous shadows spilling over the eastern border like ink on parchment.

The Waterlock Treaty had been broken—not with swords, but desperation. Farmers, priced out and ignored, had fled into forbidden lands, trying to survive. And the Outlands had answered.

The beasts didn't just attack—they erased. Coffee fields razed. Granaries gutted. Merchant wagons overturned and gutted, their horses missing, their drivers found days later with their eyes missing and limbs bent wrong.

Trade had collapsed. Gold meant nothing now. What good was coin when no ship dared enter the eastern ports? What good were royal decrees when half the eastern baronies had stopped answering them?

He'd tried to raise it at court. Tried to push the Council to act.

But Thanamalice had laughed, her wine-stained lips curled in disdain. "Let the monsters eat the poor. It's less mouths to feed."

Roman had seen then—truly seen—that the throne he'd once vowed to serve had turned to poison. And without Eleanor... there was no one left in that palace worth bleeding for.

But maybe, just maybe, there was still something worth *fighting* for.

Eleanor wasn't just his heart. She was the only one who had ever seen the rot and dared to speak against it. And if she lived—if he could find her —perhaps together they could do what this court never would.

Face the truth. Rebuild from ruin. Fight monsters with more than swords.

He stood before the open gates of Wonderworth,

flanked by the two knights he trusted most. There were no banners. No horns.

Only steel and resolve.

"Where are we bound, my prince?" one of them asked quietly.

Roman didn't hesitate this time.

"We ride east. Toward Kaerleon."

A pause.

"Do you think she'll be there?"

Roman's grip tightened on the reins. "I *hope* she is. Because if she isn't…" He looked toward the horizon, jaw set. "Then I'll search every cursed mile between here and the Outlands until I find her."

The knight nodded.

And together, they rode—into the dawn, into the broken world, and toward whatever redemption might still be carved from the ashes.

\*\*\*

Far from Wonderworth, Eleanor sat by a fountain in Kaerleon, unaware of the hooves that now pounded dry roads on her behalf.

She dipped her fingers into the water and whispered a quiet prayer to the wind—unspoken words carried off into the distance, where someone might yet be listening.

And beyond mountains, rivers, and ruined oaths,
Roman pressed forward in silence, led only by
hope.

# CHAPTER 18 - A THRONE SHARED

E leanor awoke each morning to the golden hush of Kaerleon's courtyards, where the scent of jasmine and citrus mingled in the dawn air. The days unfolded with quiet authority, her once-uncertain presence now cemented in the kingdom's lifeblood.

At King Halric's behest, she had accepted a formal title—Lady Regent of Provincial Affairs—though the people had already begun calling her something else: *Heart of Kaerleon*.

She oversaw citrus quotas and wine reserves, mediated trade disputes, and restructured caravan routes from Taryn to ensure timely harvests. In the council chamber, she spoke with clarity and conviction, earning the ear of elder merchants and young captains alike.

Gone were the shadows of her former self. And yet... the ache remained.

Halric gave her space to lead, but also to *feel*. He never pressed. Only offered, encouraged, listened.

Her private office—sunlit and carved from honeyed stone—became a sanctuary. Its shelves brimmed with scrolls from Thaloria, ledgers from Silverhaven, and even a cracked map of Wonderworth that she kept folded beneath her ink blotter.

One afternoon, after concluding a proposal to expand Kaerleon's medicinal exports, Halric closed his ledgers and leaned back in his chair beside her.

"Your plan to restock the southern granaries with Thalorian surplus passed unanimously," he said, smiling. "The council sees your foresight."

Eleanor offered a soft smile, though weariness pulled at her eyes. "Thank you, Your Majesty. I only wish I'd been able to do the same for Wonderworth... before it slipped away."

Halric's expression shifted, sympathy knitting his brow. He reached across the table and gently laid his hand over hers.

"Your love for your homeland is not weakness," he said. "It's part of what makes you so formidable. But do not let guilt eclipse the good you've done here."

Eleanor looked down at their joined hands. Her fingers curled slowly beneath his. "Your generosity humbles me, Halric. You've given me shelter... purpose... dignity. But my heart still clings to a ghost."

Halric's voice was quiet but sure. "I would never ask you to let go before you're ready. I only ask that you let me walk beside you while you heal."

That night, beneath the moon-draped colonnades, they strolled in companionable silence. Night-blooming vines whispered against the breeze as Halric paused beside a marble balustrade and turned to her.

"Tell me your burden, Eleanor," he said gently. "Let me help you carry it."

She hesitated, her breath catching.

"I fear I've misled you," she confessed. "Not by intention—but because I've tried so hard to survive, to move forward, to do right by your kindness... and yet I still dream of Wonderworth. Of what I left behind. Of someone I may never see again."

Her voice broke. "I don't know if he betrayed me. Or if I failed him. Or if fate simply played its cruel game. But I cannot forget him. Not yet."

Halric's hand reached for her chin, guiding her eyes to his. His gaze was tender.

"Eleanor," he said, "I do not love you because I expect you to forget your past. I love you because you carry it with grace. If your heart never finds its way to mine, I will still count it a blessing that you allowed me into your world."

She exhaled shakily. "I don't know what I feel. Only that I don't want to lose this. Not Kaerleon. Not you."

"Then we won't lose anything," he whispered. "Not tonight. Not tomorrow. We build what we can, day by day."

And in that moment, as he pulled her gently into an embrace, Eleanor allowed herself—for the first time—not to feel guilty for the warmth that bloomed in her chest.

At the Harvest Festival, Eleanor rode at the head of the royal procession in a gown of deep plum and embroidered gold. Banners snapped in the breeze as villagers cried her name, tossing petals beneath the hooves of the regal mounts.

Halric rode beside her, his voice low as he leaned over. "Look at them. You've given them hope."

Eleanor smiled, tears stinging her lashes. "They've

given it to me."

As the parade wound through the city, music rose like the tide. Eleanor waved to the people; the weight of her crownless station balanced by the honour she carried in their eyes.

In quiet moments, when the world stilled and the halls emptied of feasting and celebration, Halric would take her hand and whisper, "Your heart is the greatest treasure this kingdom will ever hold."

And though a part of her still longed for another voice—another promise made beneath a different moon—Eleanor found peace in this place. A different kind of love was beginning to grow, not in defiance of her past, but beside it.

# CHAPTER 19 - ASHES
# AND ECHOES

T he wind across Silverhaven carried the scent of frost and crushed lavender.

Roman stood on a high bluff overlooking pale birch forests and snow-fed lakes, his cloak snapping behind him in the wind. Wind tugged at the dark curls at his nape, throwing the outline of his sculpted shoulders into stark relief; the beard along his strong jaw bristled in the cold air, and those green eyes—sharp as flint—swept the horizon like a hunter zeroing in on his prey. The people here were distant, polished like the marble towers that dotted their capital—but cold, too.

Even with his princely seal, he was treated as no more than a foreign diplomat.

He passed through fisher villages and old merchant towns, following faint rumours of a healer with green eyes who had passed through in spring.

But when he reached the final hamlet, nestled in a glacial ravine, the name Eleanor meant nothing to anyone. There was only an old crone with poor vision and cracked hands who spoke of a dream she had—of a weeping girl in silver—but nothing more.

Roman left Silverhaven colder than when he arrived.

*** 

In Taryn, wind rippled through wide plains and golden hilltop fields.

This kingdom, so close to Wonderworth, once welcomed Roman with ceremony and song. Now, his arrival was met with wary bows and careful silences. The court had heard the rumours: that Prince Roman had lost his edge, that the heir was missing, that alliances hung by a thread.

Still, he questioned merchants at border posts, spoke to local regents, even searched among the hill shrines where fugitives were sometimes given sanctuary.

He stayed in Taryn longer than he planned.

But each thread unravelled beneath his fingers. Every sighting of "a girl with a healer's pouch" led to someone else: a Thalorian midwife, a Silverhaven trader's daughter, a grieving widow cloaked in green.

Eleanor was nowhere.

And Roman began to dream not of finding her—but of never stopping the search.

\*\*\*

In Isendra, he almost died.

The kingdom was brittle with civil unrest. Streets choked with ash and discontent. Courtyards once filled with music now rang with the sound of iron striking iron. Nobles plotted rebellions. Townsfolk hoarded grain. The border guards demanded bribes.

Roman entered disguised—no crest, no title—hoping that fewer eyes might yield better truth.

Instead, he was accused of espionage by a rival duke and imprisoned beneath the ruined Temple of Hollow Ashes. For four days he sat in a cell ankle-deep in mud, fed only brackish water and the laughter of guards.

It was a former Isendran steward, now turned jailor, who recognized him—who remembered the peace once forged between King Edgar and Isendra

—and who risked everything to set him free.

Roman fled Isendra through a drainage tunnel in the pouring rain, bloodied and burning with shame.

He didn't ask for directions. He just rode.

***

Thaloria was the worst.

It was where it began. The land of Eleanor's birth, and of her mother's exile.

Roman arrived under cover of night, traveling on foot through birch forests until he found the ruins of the cottage she had once described. There was nothing left but ivy, wild roses, and a broken hearthstone carved with a simple "Z."

He dropped to his knees before it.

He didn't pray. He just stayed there until the wind stripped the heat from his bones.

In a nearby village, a tavern keeper remembered "a quiet girl with forest eyes" who'd come seeking herbs long ago. "She left before summer," he said. "Took a boat east. Or maybe south. She was crying."

That was all.

Just tears. And departure.

Roman left Thaloria beneath a sky split with lightning.

\*\*\*

Wonderworth was the last kingdom he returned to —not for hope, but for closure.

He wandered its quieter borders. Spoke with guards who remembered Eleanor's rise and disappearance. He visited Zara's grave and laid a sprig of mountain heather on the stone, then walked the ramparts of his father's abandoned fortress, where vines overtook the battlements.

No one knew where Eleanor had gone.

Only that she had left.

And maybe—just maybe—taken his heart with her.

\*\*\*

Now five kingdoms lay behind him:

Wonderworth.    Thaloria.    Taryn.    Isendra. Silverhaven.

Each offered hope.
Each gave nothing back.

Only Kaerleon remained. Distant. Across the sea. A kingdom of salt winds, pale towers, and a king no one truly knew.

Roman stood beneath a starlit sky, the map of the realm rolled beneath his arm, his jaw tight and his spirit fraying.

"Eleanor…" he whispered again. Not for anyone to hear, not even the wind. Just to remind himself she had once existed.

He climbed into the saddle and turned Bayspur south.

The sea waited.

And beyond it… perhaps, so did she.

# CHAPTER 20 – OATHS IN BLOOM

The sea was steel beneath a bleeding sky.

Roman stood at the prow of the merchant galley, his cloak heavy with salt spray and his jaw set against the wind. Behind him, his most loyal knights huddled in silence—men who had crossed borders, weathered betrayal, and watched their prince slowly unravel.

The ship pitched hard to port, the waves lapping like hungry mouths against its hull. Roman didn't flinch.

This was the last journey. Kaerleon—the final

kingdom.

He had searched Taryn, Isendra, Silverhaven, Thaloria, and Wonderworth itself. He had interrogated merchants, bribed scouts, ridden until his legs gave out. And still, Eleanor eluded him like a fading star.

He gripped the rail until his knuckles whitened.

"If she's not here… then she is nowhere."

The thought hollowed him. He wasn't sure if he prayed anymore, or if he simply begged the ocean. For a sign. For forgiveness. For her.

The captain's voice called from the quarterdeck: "Kaerleon on the horizon!"

Roman's heart thundered once—then stilled.

He raised his eyes.

White towers emerged from the mist, rising like a mirage from the sea. Banners of silver waved above the distant harbour.

This was it. The last hope.

He breathed in deeply, and with one trembling hand, adjusted the pendant beneath his shirt—the one Eleanor had once kissed beneath a tree of stars.

As the ship cut through the waves toward the city's

eastern dock, Roman whispered into the wind.

"Please... be here."

Kaerleon hummed with activity beneath a sky of burnished gold. Autumn's touch crept down the palace walls as garlands of wheat, citrus blossom, and crimson ivy crowned the gates. Lanterns swung from marble archways, and minstrels rehearsed in the garden colonnades, their music weaving between the pillars like silk on the wind.

King Halric had declared a grand feast—a gesture of peace, strength, and renewal. His halls were to welcome allies from across the fractured kingdoms: Thaloria's envoys, Isendran artisans, Silverhaven's glassblowers, and cautious emissaries from Taryn. Wonderworth had sent no one.

Within the Great Hall, the marble floor gleamed beneath towers of polished glass and chandeliers shaped like flowering trees. Banners bearing Kaerleon's sigil—silver waves beneath silver-barked trees—draped the columns like flowing tapestries. Rows of tables bore roasted pheasant, pomegranate-laced breads, glazed root vegetables, and honeyed wines.

Eleanor, dressed in a rose-pink gown embroidered with copper leaves, moved with quiet purpose through the space. She coordinated seating charts, ensured the merchants of Taryn were not placed beside Silverhaven's icy nobles, and spoke soothingly to nervous Isendrans who feared they might be accused of espionage at any moment.

Here, she was not a displaced princess. She was a sovereign in all but name.

Halric watched her from the dais with something like reverence. In recent months, she had rebuilt his trade routes, restructured his famine aid, and softened the bitterness of court politics with charm and precision.

That afternoon, they took tea in the rose pavilion, a crescent of quiet stone beneath flowering arches.

"The silver citrus harvest exceeded our projections," Eleanor said, sipping from her cup. "The Thalorian traders will be pleased."

Halric smiled gently, his hand brushing hers. "Kaerleon thrives because you lead it. I say it without flattery."

She looked away, then met his gaze with quiet honesty. "You've given me a place to belong again. But a piece of me… still aches elsewhere."

"I know," he said, without bitterness. "And I would never ask you to pretend otherwise."

He paused. Then: "But I will ask you something else."

Eleanor's breath caught slightly.

Halric continued, "You've brought peace where there was tension, hope where there was loss. I have come to rely on your judgment, your strength, and your heart. Let me be more than your king. Be mine, Eleanor. Stand beside me—not as a guest, but as a queen."

Silence bloomed around them.

Eleanor looked at him for a long moment. Images flashed through her mind—his kindness, his patience, the steady way he never tried to possess her, only support her. He had asked nothing of her, expected nothing. But given everything.

She nodded slowly, eyes shining. "Yes," she said. "Yes, I will."

Halric reached for her hand. They rose together, the breeze stirring the petals at their feet.

They walked through the garden, under an archway of blooming nightshade and starlight roses. Lanterns glowed like captured moons. He stopped near the edge of the reflecting pool, turned to her, and kissed her.

It was not a kiss of fire—but of steadiness. A kiss that said, "I see you, I choose you, I will not falter."

And for the first time since everything shattered, Eleanor let herself believe she could open her heart again.

She didn't know what would come next. But for now, it was enough to feel peace.

Halric gently touched her cheek and smiled. "Go now," he said softly. "Get ready. Look radiant tonight. Let the court see the queen you've become."

Eleanor nodded, her heart steady, and turned toward the palace to prepare for the feast.

# CHAPTER 21 – BENEATH LANTERN LIGHT

E leanor sat before the mirror in her chamber, fingertips resting lightly on her lips. The kiss lingered there—not in heat or urgency, but in weight. It had been gentle. Steady. Kind. It had felt... safe.

And yet.

Her reflection didn't lie. Behind the soft rose of her cheeks and the faint shimmer in her eyes was a question she couldn't quite name.

*Why do I feel like I'm watching my life from outside it?*

Halric had asked her with grace. He had never pressed, never assumed. He had given her purpose, space, and healing. And she *did* feel something for him. She admired him. Trusted him. Even felt warmth in his presence.

But love?

*Is this what love feels like when it's no longer wild? When it's calm, and planned, and quietly unfolding instead of crashing through the gates of your heart?*

She thought of Roman—the chaos he'd brought, the fire in his laugh, the reckless devotion in his eyes. The pain. The silence. The way he'd vanished when she had needed him most. And yet… she had loved him with everything she was. Maybe still did.

She let out a breath, low and steady. *I said yes. And I will honor it. He deserves that. A kingdom deserves that. With time, maybe… maybe the ache will fade, and something whole will grow in its place.*

The door creaked open. Her maid, Lysa, entered with a bundle of gowns and a warm smile.

"Your Grace," she said, already curtsying though Eleanor had never insisted on such formality. "The Queen's suite is ready. Shall we dress you for the feast?"

Eleanor blinked at the title. It still didn't quite fit. "Yes," she said softly. "Help me choose."

Lysa laid out the gowns—gold silk threaded with periwinkle, a gown of midnight velvet with pearl clasps, and another: a deep green creation with copper detailing, like vines etched in flame across a forest.

"That one," Eleanor said, touching the green fabric. "It feels... strong."

"A queen's color," Lysa approved. "But first, the bath. It's been drawn."

Eleanor nodded, rising. As she stepped into the antechamber, steam curled through the air, fragrant with orange blossom and cedarwood. Lysa slipped the gown from her shoulders and guided her to the bath.

The water welcomed her with warmth. Eleanor sank into it slowly, letting it cradle her.

She closed her eyes.

*This is my life now. This is peace. This is what I chose.*

She whispered it to herself, over and over, as if repetition could make it truer.

***

In the gardens, under fading light, King Halric remained seated at the marble table, the jasmine above him still sweet on the air. His fingers traced the rim of Eleanor's abandoned teacup.

He smiled faintly.

The kiss had not been one of passion—but it had been *right*. She had not pulled away. Her eyes had shone. She had said *yes*. And Halric, who had known solitude for too long, let himself feel the full, hopeful weight of that answer.

*She will be my queen.*

It was not only her beauty that had moved him, nor her tact, nor her clever mind—though she possessed all three in abundance. It was her resilience. The way she had bent, but never broken. The way she had taken tragedy and turned it into purpose.

He imagined her beside him at council. At festivals. In the quiet hours after the court had slept. He imagined her carrying their child—Kaerleon's future growing steady and strong within her. The image softened him.

*We will build something new. Something lasting.*

And if her heart still held shadows of another, he would not fear them. He would earn her love, day by day. Not through grand promises, but through constancy. The way he always had.

He rose, straightening his coat. The sky above had turned to dusk, lanterns now glowing between branches like watchful stars.

Tonight, she would sit beside him, and the court would see.

Eleanor of Thaloria. His queen.

***

As she disappeared through the garden doors, Halric lingered beneath the archway. A footman approached with urgency.

"Your Majesty," the man said, bowing low, "an

unexpected guest has arrived. Prince Roman of Wonderworth."

Halric's expression did not falter, but the light in his eyes cooled. "Escort him to the garden. I will receive him here."

As the footman departed, Halric remained alone beneath the jasmine-covered arch, the scent sweet and cloying around him. He looked out toward the fading sun and let the silence wrap around him.

His thoughts churned.

Roman. Eleanor.


Pieces long scattered now moved into place. Her arrival in Kaerleon. Her guarded grief. The pendant she sometimes wore and quickly hid. The way her eyes flinched—just slightly—at the name Wonderworth. And now, this prince, showing up unannounced, weather-worn and desperate.

It wasn't difficult to put the pieces together.

Halric's jaw tightened. He wasn't a fool.

He had just proposed to a woman whose heart might still belong to another.

Still, he breathed deeply, steadying himself. Whatever storm was coming, he would face it with dignity.

Moments later, beneath the same jasmine-covered

arch, Prince Roman stepped forward from the shadows of the garden gate. His cloak was travel-worn, his face hollow from weeks on the road. He bowed low.

"Your Majesty. I come in peace."

Halric's brow lifted, though his voice remained steady. "Prince Roman. You honour Kaerleon. I trust the seas did not devour you before you found our shores."

Roman's voice was rough with fatigue. "They tried. But I had… reason to endure."

Halric gestured to a bench of pale stone. "Sit. Speak. There is time before the feast."

They sat in flickering silence as the breeze tugged at the lanterns. Halric poured him a cup of tea.

Roman stared into it. "I've ridden across Taryn. Through the stormed cities of Isendra. Over the cliffs of Silverhaven. I stood in Eleanor's birthplace in Thaloria. I traced every path I thought she might take. And found nothing but dust."

His hand trembled.


Halric did not speak. His jaw clenched faintly, but his gaze held only empathy.

Roman looked up. "I thought I'd gone mad. Or cursed. But someone at a Thalorian port said a ship sailed west… toward Kaerleon. So I came. Not to claim her. Just to know."

Halric rose slowly, folding his hands behind his back. His tone was quiet. "You are a guest in Kaerleon. Rest tonight. Let no grief pass your lips before bread and drink have filled you. My stewards will bring you new garments."

Roman nodded, his shoulders sagging. "Thank you."

Two palace servants appeared silently. They bowed and guided Roman away toward a secluded guest wing.

Left alone, Halric let out a slow breath. His fingers gripped the edge of the pavilion's marble table as he stared into the garden.

He is here. And now, she must choose.

# CHAPTER 22 – A
# KINGDOM BELOW

Roman reclined by the arched window of his newly assigned chamber, high in the eastern wing of Kaerleon's palace. Lanterns flickered below like fireflies among the white towers, while the vast expanse of the kingdom stretched out beyond—orchards and silver-barked forests, sunlit fields and winding rivers that shone with promise even at night.

He traced the distant hills with his gaze, heart both lifted by the realm's beauty and heavy with longing. *Could she walk those groves?* he wondered, imagining Eleanor among the orange trees, her laughter echoing like summer wind through the leaves.

Yet doubt gnawed at him: *Is she here—near enough to call my name? Or does she remain hidden, beyond my reach?* He pressed a hand to the cool glass, every breath a prayer for her safety and desire for her presence.

The chamber's high ceilings arched overhead, tapestries depicting Kaerleon's founding glinting in the lantern light. Roman felt small against such grandeur, a prince still seeking the love he had lost. *If she is not here...* the thought struck like a blade. *Then where does my path lead?* The world beyond Wonderworth and Kaerleon seemed too vast to navigate without her.

He rose and crossed to the ornate desk, quill in trembling hand, ready to draft letters to every corner of the realm. But the emptiness of the blank parchment mirrored his own uncertainty.

*Soon*, he resolved, *I face the feast—and at last, maybe I will see her again.* The night deepened, and Roman, alone in the high chamber, awaited dawn's reckoning with a heart fraught with hope and fear.

## The Feast Evening

Dawn's promise had given way to dusk's anticipation. Roman descended the grand staircase, now clad in fine garments provided by Halric's servants: a doublet of deep navy embroidered with silver thread and trousers of soft velvet. As he stepped into the Great Hall, the scents of roasted meats and spiced wines enveloped him.

King Halric greeted him at the entrance, extending an arm. "Roman, welcome. Tonight, we celebrate our bonds and welcome every friend of Kaerleon."

He shepherded Roman through clusters of nobles and merchants: Duke Harron of Thaloria, whose leather boots still bore forest soil; Lady Isara of Silverhaven, pearls in her hair and seafoam-green eyes; and Chancellor Brenn, his fingers stained with ink from treaty scrolls. Each bowed and offered a warm word, making Roman feel both a guest and an equal.

Tables groaned under platters of pheasant glazed with orange honey, steaming bowls of saffron rice, platters of citrus-marinated fish, and fresh breads still warm from the ovens. Servants moved gracefully, refilling goblets of lavender wine before the guests even noticed.

Roman sampled each delicacy, savoring flavors unfamiliar to Wonderworth's coarse fare. He laughed at an anecdote told by Kaerleon's ambassador—a tale of marsh revelries—and found himself almost believing he could remain here forever.

Yet beneath the revelry, Roman's heart simmered

with unrest. *If only Eleanor were here,* he thought as he raised his glass to Halric. *I would stay without question.* But his lips pressed into a firm line; without her, even this paradise felt hollow.

Halric noticed the fleeting shadow across Roman's face. "You seem miles away, old friend," he said quietly, guiding Roman to a quieter alcove.

Roman sighed, gaze sweeping the jubilant throng. "This kingdom—its beauty, its prosperity—it humbles me. But I cannot enjoy it fully while my heart lies elsewhere."

Halric clasped his shoulder with quiet empathy. "Soon, you will find what you seek. And then, perhaps, you will taste these joys fully. Tonight, let us celebrate hope—hope that all wounds may heal."

They raised their goblets together, the hall's music swelling in a hopeful refrain. Roman drank deeply, eyes alight with determination: his search, his love, and his destiny awaited under Kaerleon's starlit sky.

*** 

As the final chords of the minstrels faded into polite chatter, a ripple of expectation swept through the Great Hall. Chandeliers glittered overhead, and even the flicker of candlelight seemed to pause.

Roman's gaze flared; he felt every heartbeat

echoing in his ears. He straightened, shoulders squared, as the murmur around him hushed to a whisper. Servants froze mid-step, goblets poised at trembling lips, and noble eyes turned toward the staircase.

At the summit, Eleanor appeared—an ethereal vision framed by moonlit silk. Her gown of midnight velvet cascaded like a waterfall of stars, the silver vines woven into its fabric catching the light with each gentle sway. A circlet of silver rested upon her brow, and her dark hair tumbled in soft waves across her shoulders.

A collective breath was held as she moved, each footfall measured and serene. The marble steps reflected her silhouette in pale light, and for Roman, time seemed to slow to a heartbeat.

He pushed through the crowd, other courtiers parting before him as though guided by unseen hands. Every step throbbed with anticipation as he closed the distance: the scrape of his boots on polished stone, the soft murmur of curious voices, the rise and fall of his own breath.

His eyes never left Eleanor's form—scanning the familiar curve of her cheek, the tremor of her lips, the way her hands gripped the banister. Doubt evaporated in that instant; months of searching, of pain and uncertainty, crystallized into this one miraculous moment.

He reached the base of the stair just as she paused, her gaze lifting to meet his. A single glance passed between them—intense, electric, a silent confession of longing and relief.

Roman dropped to one knee, heart pounding like war drums. "Eleanor," he whispered, voice thick with emotion, "after all this time... you stand before me."

Silence reigned as the assembled guests watched, rapt, breathless. Roman rose, stepping forward until only a breath separated them.

He reached for her hand, trembling, and lifted it to his lips with reverent care. The hall seemed to hold its breath, every candle flame flickering in unison.

\*\*\*

Two men.

Two hearts laid bare.

One word could bind her to the crown of Kaerleon; another could shatter every allegiance she's made. Will Eleanor honor her promise to a king who sheltered her... or risk it all to follow the love that calls her name? The choice hangs between them, and the next part will reveal which path her heart will claim.

# A Letter From Winter

**Dear Reader,**

Thank you—from the very bottom of my heart—for choosing to read *Where the Crown Fell*. This story has lived inside me for many years, and to see it finally out in the world, in your hands and in your heart, is a dream come true.

This is my very first novel as a self-published author, and your support means more than I can express. Whether you were swept away by Eleanor and Roman's journey, intrigued by the courtly power plays, or enchanted by the magic woven through the kingdoms, I'm truly grateful you joined me on this adventure.

If you enjoyed the book, I would be incredibly thankful if you could leave a review on Amazon. Not only does it help others discover the story, but as a new author, your feedback is especially valuable to me. It helps me grow, improve, and shape the stories I'll tell next.

Your words have power. Even a few lines make a

difference.

With all my gratitude,

**Winter Warleggan**

Author of *Where the Crown Fell*

https://www.winterwarleggan.uk

# Acknowledgement

## Continue the Journey...

Thank you for reading Where the Crown Fell—a tale of love, sacrifice, and destiny in a world of kings, queens, and magic. This story would not have come to life without the unwavering support and encouragement I received along the way. A heartfelt thank you to Charlotte Lings and Jamielee Birch for their valuable feedback—you helped shape this book in ways I'll always be grateful for.

To everyone who believed in me, cheered me on, and reminded me to keep writing even when it felt impossible—thank you. Your belief lit the path to this moment. The journey doesn't end here.

Stay tuned for Book Two, where hearts will clash, kingdoms will tremble, and the crown's true weight will be tested.

# WHERE THE CROWN ROSE

### Book Two of the Saga

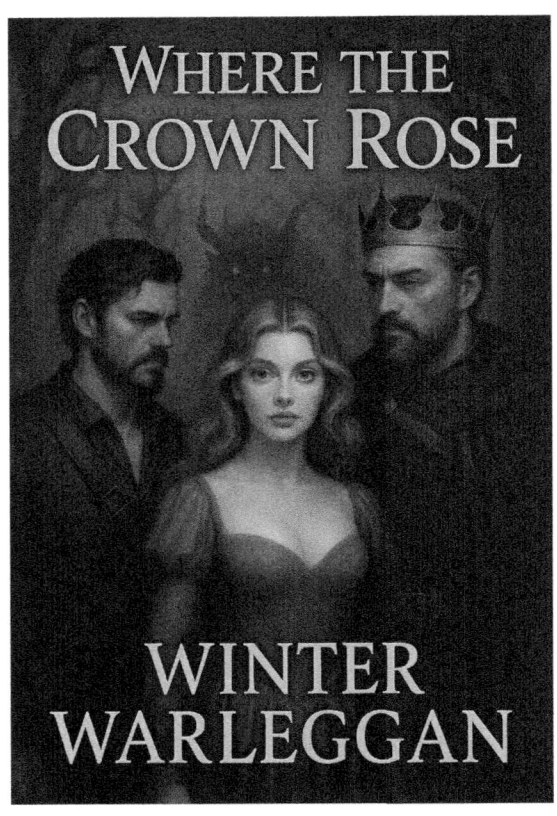

# Prologue

They buried the king in silence.

No public procession. No mourning bells.

No banners draped the palace gates.

The death of King Edgar of Wonderworth was treated like a weathered painting quietly removed from the gallery walls—forgotten before it was missed.

Queen Thanamalice made sure of it.

She stood alone in the chapel crypt beneath the palace, watching as the stone lid was sealed over the casket. The torchlight behind her flickered, stretching her shadow long against the cold marble floor. The priest dared not speak. The guards dared not breathe.

There would be no national day of mourning. No tearful tributes from foreign courts. To announce Edgar's passing was to announce a vacancy—an opportunity.

And Thanamalice did not believe in leaving doors open.

She pressed her gloved hand against the lid and whispered, "Sleep well, old fool. You ruled with your heart. And look what it cost you."

Behind her, the first council meeting without him had already begun.

# CHAPTER 1 – CRACKS
# IN THE CROWN

**W**onderworth stank of rot.

Not of the flesh—yet—but of politics. Of whispers too bold for the corridors and too sharp for the throne room. Of lies dressed in velvet and oaths that tasted like ash.

From her chamber window, Princess Nerezza looked out at the city and saw not the glinting rooftops of her birthright but a sinking ship. Fires burned in the southern quarter where grain riots had erupted the night before. Soldiers now lined the markets, but the crowds had grown hungry and restless. Wagons carrying bread were overturned before sunrise. The palace steward had taken three knives in the back just trying to negotiate wheat from the western grain barons.

And all the while, her mother smiled.

The Queen of Wonderworth was calm as ever, seated at the long obsidian table of the royal council chamber, flanked by aging advisors too afraid to question her commands. She wore her widowhood like a coronation robe—jet-black silk trimmed in silver thorns, no veil, no tears.

Nerezza paced the gallery above, watching it unfold.

"You should be down there," she muttered aloud. "Father would've wanted you to show your face. To steady the court."

But Thanamalice did not believe in steadiness.

She believed in storms.

Below, Lord Verrick stood from his seat, voice trembling. "Your Majesty, the western provinces are threatening to withhold taxes unless you publicly name an heir."

"I have named an heir," Thanamalice replied, eyes never lifting. "You are standing beneath her."

Nerezza turned from the railing, her breath catching.

She had been waiting for those words. Had bled for them. Had watched Eleanor Labrelle steal whispers and attention while she'd remained loyal, poised, perfect. And now, at last, the kingdom would see it.

Nerezza of Wonderworth. The next queen.

But the moment of triumph was already splintering.

Another voice rose—Lady Solenna, sharp-eyed and unafraid. "With respect, your Majesty, the people may not accept your daughter without the king's formal seal. And the seal has... disappeared."

Thanamalice looked up slowly.

"It will be found."

Nerezza felt the shift. That thread of ice winding through her spine.

She knew what came next.

She left the gallery without waiting for the end of the meeting.

In the hall outside, the air was thick with smoke from the braziers. Courtiers moved quickly now—quietly—muttering between tapestries and alcoves. The usual perfume of the court was now laced with sweat and the acrid sting of fear.

A page ran past her, clutching a scroll. Another limped behind him, his cheek freshly bruised.

No one said it aloud, but all knew: the court had become a prison with gowns instead of bars.

And in the west—beyond the Outlands, beyond the dead king's shadow—a girl they had buried in scandal now stood on Kaerleon's marble floors.

The bastard had returned.

Nerezza didn't know how. Didn't know why. But she could feel it.

Eleanor's breath was still warm in the world.

And nothing made the wolves hungrier than the scent of a rival reborn.

Printed in Dunstable, United Kingdom

63572622R00119